I0727130

THE HOUSEWIFE ASSASSIN'S HUSBAND HUNTING HINTS

JOSIE BROWN

keeping tips at the start of each chapter—each with its own deadly twist! This book is perfect for relaxing in the bath with after a long day. I can't wait to read the next in the series. Highly Recommended!"

—*CrimeThrillerGirl.com*

"This was an addictive read—gritty but funny at the same time. I ended up reading it in just one evening and couldn't go to sleep until I knew what the outcome would be! It was action-packed and humorous from the start, and that continued throughout, I was pleased to discover that this is the first of a series and look forward to getting my hands on Book Two so I can see where life takes Donna and her family next!"

—*Me, My Books, and I*

"The two halves of Donna's life make sense. As you follow her story, there's no point where you think of her as "Assassin Donna" vs. "Mummy Donna', her attitude to life is even throughout. I really like how well this is done. And as for Jack. I'll have one of those, please?"

—*The Northern Witch's Book Blog*

Novels in The Housewife Assassin Series

The Housewife Assassin's Handbook (Book 1)

The Housewife Assassin's Guide to Gracious Killing (Book 2)

The Housewife Assassin's Killer Christmas Tips (Book 3)

The Housewife Assassin's Relationship Survival Guide (Book 4)

The Housewife Assassin's Vacation to Die For (Book 5)

The Housewife Assassin's Recipes for Disaster (Book 6)

The Housewife Assassin's Hollywood Scream Play (Book 7)

The Housewife Assassin's Killer App (Book 8)

The Housewife Assassin's Hostage Hosting Tips (Book 9)

The Housewife Assassin's Garden of Deadly Delights (Book 10)

The Housewife Assassin's Tips for Weddings, Weapons, and Warfare (Book 11)

The Housewife Assassin's Husband Hunting Hints (Book 12)

The Housewife Assassin's Ghost Protocol (Book 13)

The Housewife Assassin's Terrorist TV Guide (Book 14)

The Housewife Assassin's Deadly Dossier (Book 15: The Series Prequel)

The Housewife Assassin's Greatest Hits (Book 16)

The Housewife Assassin's Fourth Estate Sale (Book 17)

The Housewife Assassin's Horrorscope (Book 18)

First Comes Love, then Comes Marriage

To demonstrate your total commitment to each other, you and your mister tied the knot! (And lo and behold, it wasn't around his neck—literally, if not metaphorically.)

However, should it turn out that his idea of marital bliss differs substantially from yours, these tips will bring you two lovebirds back together (without knocking heads):

First, should a conflict arise, listen to his rationale as to why his way is better than yours. As you listen, be silent, smile, and nod.

Next, when he is done, it's your turn. As with a four-year-old, simply saying, "No—because I say so," should suffice.

Finally, if he insists on further debate of the issue, a rock salt blast at twelve feet from your trusty shotgun should preclude any further negotiation. From now on, "Because I say so," should yield the Pavlovian response it deserves: complete obedience. Talk about a happily-ever-after ending!

"Just tell me what it will take to get my husband back." I refuse to cry while I'm on the phone with Eric Webber, leader of the international terrorist group known as the Quorum and the son of a bitch who kidnapped Jack.

"But, I have told you, my dear."

By that he means I'm to be a pawn for the Quorum.

A paid killer for a terrorist organization.

A traitor to my country.

Despite knowing that every second matters if I'm to get the hell out of this honeymoon suite and track down Eric's operatives, I count to ten. Finally: "Okay, I'm in."

"Easier said than done," he warns me. "There will be a series of initiation tests. Should you pass them, your husband lives."

Click.

As I stare down at the one clue Jack left me—a bloody button, torn from the shirt he wore when he walked out the door, I think, *What have I done?*

Hopefully, I've given Jack a chance to survive until I find him.

Or perhaps, a chance to escape.

In the meantime, I am married to the Quorum.

At least, that's what I'll let Eric think.

I presume I'm being watched and heard, to see what I'll do next. Will I call Acme Industries, the black-ops company that both Jack and I work for?

Or will I try to run out of the room in search of Jack?

Neither. Instead, my eyes scan for anything that could pass for a webcam—for example, a digital eye in hanging art, or a camera hidden in an overhead light fixture or an alarm clock. Or perhaps there's a camera staring out at me from the glass-fronted mini-bar.

A full sweep of the room pulls up nothing.

Is there a camera hidden inside the television? I move an ottoman in front of the TV, then lift my suitcase and place it on top of it. I open the lid so that it blocks the television screen.

Even if the Quorum operatives weren't able to get a camera in the room, they might have planted an audio bug. I go into the bathroom and turn on the shower—

Before slipping out the balcony door.

The room has a spectacular view of the Pacific Ocean. Gentle waves roll onto an empty beach. Lights from a few boats dot the black water under an indigo sky.

My hotel room is on the third floor. If those shadowing me are next door, I can only go down.

I drop onto the balcony below.

Like our suite, this room has two sliding doors—one to the bedroom, another to the living room.

The good news: one is unlocked.

The bad news: it's the bedroom door.

Even worse news: a couple is thrashing around on the bed, in the throes of passion.

I'm being polite when I say that the woman is riding high in the saddle. Between her highs and lows, her grunts and groans, a stream of dirty words spews from her pursed lips.

While she's being satisfied by her partner's most essential appendage of the moment, each of his other four is shackled to the nearest bedpost. The man's eyes open wide when he sees me crossing the room toward the hallway. But, with a silk scarf tied over his mouth, all he can do is grunt out his shock and indignation.

The woman takes it as tacit approval that she's saying all the right things. By the time I'm out the door, she's turned into a real potty mouth.

It's not our form of love play, but to each their own.

Right now, I'd give anything to feel Jack's arms around me.

I run down the hall to the fire exit that leads out to the side of the building.

THE KID AT THE RECEPTION DESK IN THE HOTEL LOBBY IS TOO busy texting his buddy to see me make my way into the general manager's office.

It takes me just a few seconds to pick the lock.

The desk is cluttered with files. I have to push some aside in order to find the general manager's nametag:

Tommy Scott. From the number of boards hanging on the walls, apparently, Tommy is a surfer dude from way back. His personal photos in the frames scattered on top of the credenza and on numerous file cabinets throughout the room move through his life progression: from a bronzed flaxen-haired Samson in a wetsuit, to a paunchy leathery balding Boomer in a Hawaiian shirt.

There are no pictures of a wife or kids, just a Labrador retriever: first as a puppy, then aged, to the point of having a gray, grizzled snout. I squint to read the dog's tag, which is visible in the closest picture. It reads *Maui*. Scrawled on the photo is:

RIP 2015

It takes me about a minute to figure out the password to the laptop. First I try *Maui2015*, but it doesn't work. Next I try *SurfsUp*. Still nothing.

WipeOut does the trick.

Yikes. If Tommy's password is indicative of his self-esteem, I'd hate to be his shrink.

The security camera's app is sitting right on the computer's desktop. It launches with a click. Immediately, the lobby comes into view. The kid at the front desk is just as I left him: comatose, except for his fingers, which tap away at his text. I guess at the command to bring up the videos on the various floors. Since Jack and I are on the third floor, I hit the number 3.

Bingo.

The screen changes to the hallway outside our door, in real time. The back command button rewinds the video feed.

I stop it when I see Jack.

He is being pushed into a hotel laundry cart by a woman dressed as a housekeeper and a large broad-shouldered man in his mid-thirties with a swarthy complexion. His head is shaved. The woman is perhaps in her late twenties, a pretty girl with sultry features: a broad forehead, almond eyes, and olive complexion. Her long dark hair is loose to her shoulders. Both are Latino, no doubt.

Jack is bleeding. Why? How? Is it a fatal wound? I can't tell at this angle.

I rewind it further, to the exact moment in which the first person enters the previously empty hall. It is the housekeeper. She enters via the elevator and stops outside the doorway exactly across from ours, but she doesn't go in. When she nods, I presume it's because her partner has just said something to her via an earpiece.

As Jack comes out of our room, she turns slightly and picks up a stack of bath towels. By the time he's next to the cart, they've made eye contact. He nods. She smiles. She holds out the towels.

Her offer takes him off his guard. He smiles back and says something as he takes them.

The moment his arms are full, she stabs him in the neck with a syringe.

Jack refuses to go down without a fight. He takes the

cart between them and shoves it into her so hard that she hits the back of her head against the wall.

He stumbles to get back into our room—

But he doesn't make it. Her companion comes flying out of the hotel room across from ours. He carries a gun.

Thank God the man doesn't shoot Jack with it, but he hits him over the head.

Instinctively, Jack's hand reaches for the wound. As he draws his hand away, he sees that it is covered in blood. He takes a step toward the man, only to succumb to the drug now coursing through his veins.

His hand swipes at the wall, leaving a smear of blood.

By now, the woman has regained her footing. The man angrily motions at her to help him drop Jack into the cart. She then scurries to pick up the towels that are now scattered throughout the hall, and tosses them into the cart with Jack.

My husband's kidnappers roll him down the hall, into the service elevator.

For Jack's captors, it is an interminable wait before the elevator doors open. I realize this when the man anxiously slams his fist hard and fast against the button, as if this will improve its speed.

I stare at the cart on the screen, ashamed that I lay in the blissful afterglow of sex while Jack struggled for his life.

Finally, the doors open.

They shove the cart into the elevator. They stand in

front of it, prepared to block it from the view of anyone else who might enter.

I switch to the elevator camera, rewinding to a few seconds before they enter it.

The camera's eye is directly overhead. Because of this, the housekeeper and her henchman don't see what I do: Jack's arm rising from the cart.

He drops something.

I found it: the bloody button from the shirt he wore out the door.

The time stamp shows eighteen minutes ago.

I shift to another camera—the one in the lobby—and rewind to the same time stamp. When the elevator door opens, the housekeeper hauls the cart in the direction of a service hallway, while her companion walks out the hotel's front door, just as carefree as can be.

I now switch my view to a camera that covers the back of the hotel. The housekeeper stands near the service entrance. A moment later, her henchman drives up in an unmarked white service van. Together, they haul the cart up the van's back ramp.

I zoom in on the license plate and write it down.

When the van pulls out of the parking lot, it turns right onto the Pacific Coast Highway.

South.

I copy the digital files I've just seen, along with any files beginning with Jack's and my arrival at the hotel, sending them to a secure data cloud I set up several years ago under my Aunt Phyllis's name. Thank goodness

Phyllis is a Luddite when it comes to anything other than the poker game app on her cellphone.

Afterward, I delete the same data files on Tommy's computer, as well as those on the hotel's account to the cloud where its files are uploaded.

I then delete the webcam app. By the time Tommy loads it back into his computer, I'll be long gone.

I'm about to head out the door when I hear someone coming. I duck below the desk and ease myself under the credenza.

The door opens. It's the housekeeper.

She rushes toward the desk and plops down in front of the computer. She had the same idea as me, only her goal is to delete the files. It's doubtful that Tommy or anyone else on his staff will take the time to peruse them if there are no guest complaints filed prior to its seven-day auto-deletion, but she's not taking any chances.

Well, neither am I.

She's too busy clicking away in a desperate attempt to find the webcam app to hear me as I rise silently behind her. I take the pristine letter opener off Tommy's credenza. I will stab her, but in some place that won't kill her.

I need to keep her alive, if only to torture her to find out where the Quorum has taken Jack.

I'm just about to strike when she stops clicking. I realize why when our eyes meet in the reflection on the computer screen.

Before I can stab her, she elbows me in the gut.

When I double over, she reaches across the desk, pulling the scissors from the pencil cup.

This gives me time to jab her thigh.

She yelps and leaps straight up—

Into my sidekick.

It slams her into the wall that holds the surfboards. One clatters to the floor, barely missing her head.

She picks it up and runs at me, swinging at my head.

I duck just in time.

Before she has time to swing again, I jab at her once more with the letter opener.

She blocks it with the surfboard and it sticks in the damn thing!

Realizing this, she smiles triumphantly. She swings it at me again, but this time she flings the board high over her head in an attempt to crack my noggin—

Ain't happening.

I charge her, head-butting her in the stomach.

Doubling over, she drops the surfboard.

I catch it.

It makes a great bat. I catch the back of her head just as she tries to right herself. She goes down face first, cracking her head on the edge of Tommy's desk before slamming into the hardwood floor.

Oh, hell.

I feel for a pulse—

Nothing.

Shit.

A cellphone is buzzing. It's somewhere on her body.

Frantically, I search her uniform for pockets. I find the right one, under her apron on her right hip.

Thank goodness it's a text message, not a call.

It's in Spanish: *Dónde estás?*

Ah. He asks, *Where are you?*

I can read Spanish *un poquito* (a little) but writing it? *Ay, caramba!*

Not to panic. I pull out my own cellphone and hit the translator app. My answer:

Limpiando. ¡Ja! La esposa perra es un desastre. Ella está en la ducha, llorando como un bebé. Tenga cuidado de los negocios sin mí. Me pondré al día en 24 horas.

Translation:

Cleaning up. Ha! His bitch wife is a mess. She is in the shower, crying like a baby. Take care of business without me. I'll catch up in 24 hours.

A moment later her accomplice texts back: *OK.*

Now, just one more task before I take out the trash: I scan the security system's QR code so that I can remotely access the camera feed with my cellphone, and then I split the feed so that anyone else accessing this feed sees a loop of archival footage taken from the twenty-four hour period prior to Jack's kidnapping. That way, no one sees my comings and goings, yet I see the real thing, in real time.

Finally, I lift her from under her arms and drag her out of the office. Something falls out of her pocket: her master key card. I take it. Maybe I can peek inside my surveillance team's room while they're napping, or out by the pool.

Conveniently, she left the laundry cart outside the door. I shove her into it and head down the hallway.

Time for us to take a joy ride.

The front desk kid doesn't look up as I wheel the cart past him toward the service door.

One of the hotel's amenities is a pier, where a couple of sailboats and a small skiff with an outboard motor are tethered for guest use.

After heaving the housekeeper into the skiff, I set sail. I go far enough out to sea that should her body find its way to shore, it'll be much further down the coast.

Is that where they've taken Jack?

Had I kept her alive, I might have my answer.

Too late now.

Over the side she goes.

The housekeeper's body bobs twice above the waves before slipping under the frothy chop. At that second, I wish I could conjure her from the dead in order to ask her.

Hell, I've just made a pact with the Devil, so maybe I can.

Before Eric or another of his operatives discovers me missing from the room, I have one more stop to make:

I must find Ryan Clancy, my boss at Acme Industries, where both Jack and I work.

I'll head over to the office on the off-chance that he may actually be there.

Black-ops organizations aren't like other companies, with a human resources director who coordinates a personnel directory containing everyone's home address and telephone number. It would certainly have made it easier for sending out my wedding invitations.

Or, for that matter, those for a funeral.

I won't let my mind go there.

Never.

But before I find Ryan, I have to ask myself: how much can I tell him without jeopardizing Jack's life?

2

Honesty Is Always the Best Policy!

Helpful hint to husbands: when it comes to couples communication, total and complete truthiness must be adhered to—

Despite the consequences.

For example:

Even if the iron is within tossing distance, it behooves you to answer yes when she asks, "Do I look fat in this dress?" Granted, you'll be in a coma for at least a few days after it hits your face, but isn't it worth it if she is saved from the giggles and eye-rolls that undoubtedly would have come her way had she not been at your hospital bedside? Someday she will thank you for taking it on the chin, quite literally.

Another example:

You've been out drinking with your buddies when you told her you were working late. Since you reek of liquor, your option now is to (A) fudge and say your boss invited you out for a drink; (B) lie and say someone at work opened a bottle of champagne to celebrate a big account acquisition; or (C) tell the truth.

If you think either A or B will do because they are, at worst, little white lies, think again. Only the truth will set you free.

Well, that, and a good lawyer who can document spousal abuse.

JACK'S CAR IS IN THE HOTEL'S PARKING LOT. KNOWING IT'S being watched, I steal another car from down the block: a ubiquitous black Lexus with darkened windows. Perfect.

My first stop is Acme. It's a long shot that Ryan is there, as opposed to tucked in and sound asleep in his bed. Except for the skeleton crew of handlers communicating with field agents on active missions, just two hours ago, he, along with a majority of Acme's operatives, were partying down at our wedding.

I access Acme via the tunnel leading to an underground garage positioned directly under its headquarters building. I don't use my access code or even Jack's, but that of our debonair British associate, Dominic Fleming. He divulged it to me one evening when he was too drunk to drive his Aston Martin home, and asked me to do so for him.

I smear the tunnel and garage's security cameras with

grime so that images are blurred. I've only got twenty minutes, tops, before Acme security notices, so I'd better move fast.

Dominic's code is *Perfect1*. Wishful thinking, but hey, we all need goals in life.

As I suspected, Ryan's car is nowhere in sight. Despite this, it's worth it for me to break into his office so that I may find some clue as to where he lives. He truly is an enigma. But if I'm to save Jack, I need to fill in at least that piece of the puzzle.

BEFORE MOVING INTO THE ELEVATOR IN THE UNDERGROUND parking lot, I pick the lock on the car trunk of our research director's car, Lydia Kimpton, where she keeps a few spare lab coats, shoe booties, gloves, facemasks, and bonnets, even lifting tape. She has night blindness, so I presume that after work she hitched a ride with Abu Nagashahi, the street operative who usually acts as my cutout. He hasn't noticed, but she's sweet on him. From the samba they were doing at my wedding, my guess is that he finally caught on. For both their sakes—and mine —I hope so, and that she'll be riding into work with him in the morning too.

I take what I need from her trunk. This includes the lifting tape, which I use in order to get Lydia's fingerprint off the car's steering wheel.

As I enter the building, I give a wave to a security

guard before pressing her print onto the security touch pad.

The guard waves back with barely a glance.

I'm in.

I DO MY BEST TO WALK CASUALLY THROUGH THE HANDLER PIT, toward Ryan's office. Thank goodness, the few handlers on duty don't even bother to look up. The operatives in their care are their first and only priority, as it should be.

I'm surprised that Ryan didn't lock his door. I wince at the thought that it proves he has nothing to hide, and therefore nothing to find that will help me locate him as soon as possible. The blinds to the glass wall that faces the office pit are drawn, so I won't draw attention to his office by having to do so.

The top of his mammoth-sized desk holds nothing but a Meisterstück Solitaire Blue Montblanc pen in its custom-made holder. None of the desk drawers are locked. There has to be some clue as to where he goes home at night. I'm sure it's an exercise in futility, but I try the drawers anyway.

There are two on either side off his chair and a slim but wide one in the middle, which holds his laptop. Unlike the one belonging to the hotel's general manager, Ryan's password is a ten-characters-long combination of random digits, letters, and characters. Acme passwords are changed out daily, and different for every Acme operative. All keystrokes are recorded. Should it be done in the wrong combination, the supposed hacker is automatically locked out after the third incorrect attempt, and a silent alarm is set off.

If all else fails, I'll have to try it.

First, I try the drawers to the left of the desk chair. The smaller one on the top holds a stapler, paper clips, and a few sharpened pencils. The larger drawer below it holds a bottle of scotch and a tumbler. It's half full.

No one should drink alone.

I move to the large bottom drawer on the right. Inside is a laundered shirt and roll-on deodorant. Ryan is big, hairy, and has many reasons to sweat, so no surprise there.

The top right drawer has a few lined pads, but nothing else. I flip through them, to see if he's written down anything of consequence, but all the sheets are blank.

Sort of.

If you look closely, you'll notice that the bottom pad has some faint indentations on its last page, the one next to the pad's cardboard backing. I take one of the pencils from Ryan's top drawer and rub its tip gently over the page. The images are faint, but there they are:

LQ#5N5*3BX

Is this today's code?

There is only one way to find out.

I open the drawer containing Ryan's laptop. The drawer's front panel folds down, so that when I pull it out, it is the right height for typing.

I lift the cover on his MacBook. Other than the password input bar, a black screen stares back at me. It taunts me to tap in the code.

I hesitate for two reasons. First, I don't need a phalanx of security guards storming Ryan's office and arresting me. And next, I hate being the one to shatter my boss and dear friend's privacy.

But, I have to. Jack's life is at stake.

I type in the code just as I see it written.

And wait a moment—

Before a screen-sized photo of the Lincoln memorial greets me.

I'm in.

A MULTITUDE OF FOLDERS BECKON. I DON'T RECOGNIZE THE names attached to them. I presume they are nicknames of missions or operatives.

One is labeled BLACK WIDOW.

It's mine.

To prove I'm right, I click on to it.

As I suspected, my life opens before me: Before Acme, even before Carl; my Acme missions, and the mission reports assessing them; Ryan's assessments of me, after every mission. There's much more, but as curious as I am, I realize I don't have time look through this. I have to save Jack.

To do that, I need to get up close and personal with Ryan.

So, which one holds the key to his kingdom?

I scan the names on the other files. I'm sure most of them refer to other Acme operatives, but there's got to be a file or two with some personal items—

Perhaps this one: ROSEBUD

If it's not yet another operative's dossier, it's one of two things: either Ryan is a movie buff, or he's into gardening.

I open the file. It holds a bunch of jpegs. I click on to one tagged MOLINEUX, only to find myself staring at stunningly beautiful yellow rose. The velvety folds of its petals are like nothing I've ever seen before.

It is clasped within a beefy palm—

Belonging to Ryan. I can tell from the scar on the skin between his thumb and his index finger: a souvenir from one of his First Gulf War missions.

The location's GPS coordinates are embedded in the photo's EFIX data. Hopefully, it was taken in his private garden versus on some outing.

I take the coordinates and input them into Google Earth. By zooming in, I can barely make out a rooftop through a thick copse of trees clinging to a hillside that ends in a sheer drop into the Pacific Ocean. It's about fifteen minutes from here.

In the seven years I've known him, I have never been to Ryan's home. To the best of my knowledge, neither has Jack.

Ryan Clancy is an enigma in so many ways. I'm sure he won't welcome my solving this part of his puzzling life.

Still, he loves my husband like a son. He'll understand that if I'm to save Jack, I must go to him now.

RYAN MAY LIVE IN A SMALL CABIN, BUT IT HAS THE SECURITY protocol that would shame Buckingham Palace.

Except where the property drops off an ocean cliff, a ten-foot-high chain link fence is buried deep in the high bushes that surround the perimeter of the property. With my night vision goggles, I've detected an infrared beam. It comes from a camera attached to a drone that zips over the two acres of overgrown brush and forest, assessing the thermal heat signatures of every crow, coyote, and raccoon that may wander onto it, not to mention an unin-vited human who emanates too much heat to be mistaken for a wild critter.

Believe me, I'd love it if I could simply walk up to Ryan's front gate, stick my adorable mug into the security camera, and wave at him. But given the urgency, I'm not taking any chances. I may have given the Quorum the slip, but that doesn't mean they aren't watching Ryan, his abode, or his security feed.

The drone hovers nearby, but apparently, its sensors aren't calibrated to detect motion from anywhere outside the fence.

So instead, I climb a Manzanita tree that is taller than the cabin.

I pray that the drone isn't equipped with a semi-automatic rifle too.

I chuckle at the thought.

It takes me six slow, torturous minutes to inch my way onto the thickest branch hanging over Ryan's roof. I right myself, bracing myself against the trunk.

It's going to take a flying leap onto the roof to beat detection. Then I'll have to scramble to the skylight. From what I can tell, it's the type that cranks open in order to let in fresh air. Ideally, I'll be able to slip through it, or at the very least, yell down to Ryan.

The weakness of the branch doesn't work in my favor. Already it is swaying, and it is so narrow that a misstep will send me hurtling down the rocky cliff to the beach, six stories below. Still, I'll have momentum on my side.

At least, that's what I tell myself.

I take a deep breath and gauge the number of running

strides needed for liftoff. The sharp crack of the branch beneath me tells me I have no time to waste.

Four would have been ideal, but I'm mid-air in three.

I land hard on both feet—

And come face-to-face with a raccoon.

Hissing, he raises up on his hind legs.

To make matters worse, the drone swoops overhead.

Oh, fresh hell—its beam has locked on to me!

Something emerges just below the drone's electronic eye—

The barrel of a gun.

Really, Ryan?

I have one second to do something—

It's the last thing any sane person would do: I grab the raccoon, and hold it in front of me.

The raccoon is too shocked to do anything but freeze.

It takes a bullet in the heart.

I am spattered in its blood and guts. *Pee-yoo—the smell!*

Enough of this merde. I throw the raccoon at the drone. The carcass is heavy enough that when it hits the drone, the whole mess slams downward—

Crashing through the skylight.

"What the HELL?" Ryan's voice thunders up to me.

Yikes.

I take a step backward—

Big mistake. There are so many leaves on the roof that one foot slips out from under me. The roof's pitch is steep enough to send me rolling to the edge. I grab hold of the gutter, but it breaks away from the cabin—

And I'm swinging over the cliff.

With all my might, I sway the gutter back toward the hill—

But it gives way, and I'm airborne.

I slam to the ground, and am rolling to the edge when I bump into something hard.

A gravestone.

There are fresh flowers at its base: twelve white calla lilies.

Carved into it is a name: *Natalie Lynn Bevins Clancy*

Ryan was once married? Well, what do you know?

The date of her death is four years prior to my meeting Carl.

I do the birth-to-death math in my head: she was only thirty-three when she died.

I'm still staring at it when I hear Ryan's voice behind me: *"What the hell are you, of all people, doing here?"*

I spring from the ground in order to shush him with a finger on his lips. I'll be damned if we're going to speak until we were safely inside his home, away from prying eyes (human, drone, or satellite).

He may be tired and bleary-eyed, but he gets the message. He jerks his chin toward the cabin.

I nod my thanks and start up the hill.

I'm halfway there when I realize that he isn't following. When I turn around, I see why: he's staring down at the grave.

Sadly, a couple of the flowers were crushed in my fall. He takes them, sighs, and throws them down the hill.

Yes, I feel guilty. If only I'd known of his loss.

As soon as we're on the other side of his door, my sorrow will soon have the company it craves.

There will be quid pro quo, if Ryan allows it.

"You know I wouldn't have shown up on your doorstep if it wasn't urgent." I sink into one of the two large worn leather chairs that flank the living room's fireplace. It holds ashes, long dead.

Suddenly, it dawns on me how filthy I am.

I rise, but Ryan motions me to sit down again. Realizing that I am shivering, he pokes one of the dying embers in the hearth, as if willing it to come to life. It flares just a second before accommodating his wish and warming into an amber halo.

The fire provides the only light in the room, so I can't see much. The room, small, holds a tiny dining table and a couple of straight back chairs. They are placed directly in front of the window. The drapes are drawn, so I can't see out.

A galley kitchen is on the far end of the room. Open planks, anchored onto its brick wall, act as shelving for a few cups and plates. Next to the front door, a narrow staircase leads up to the second story.

Anticipating my need to scan my surrounding, Ryan waits until my eyes move back around to him before asking, "Donna, what's happened?"

"It's Jack. He's been…kidnapped." I blink away the scrim of tears that cloud my eyes.

"Do you know by whom?"

"Yes," I nod, "the Quorum."

"I guess it Eric's way of retaliation for our taking down Eileen Woodley and Frannie."

Ryan's summation is valid, considering that Jack and I discovered that the Quorum had two operatives planted within the White House staff: President Lee Chiffray's long-time trusted secretary, and his stepdaughter Janie's nanny.

Eileen was murdered by Lee's Secret Service leader, Lurch Muldoon, as she attempted to kill me for discovering her duplicity. As for Frannie, I cornered her on the president's bedroom terrace, but I didn't take her out. That honor went to the First Lady, Babette Chiffray, when she discovered Frannie was sharing her lover: Salem Rahmin al-Sadah, the CEO of Graffias International, an international banking and software conglomerate that is really a legally-run corporation that laundered money for the Quorum.

I had already killed Salem. It's a wonder Babette didn't use that as an excuse to try to chuck me over the balcony too, considering he was the father of the child she is carrying.

I'm still not convinced that Babette isn't as big of a threat to national security as either Frannie or Eileen were. But it's something Acme will have to prove to Lee.

But first things first: I must save Jack.

Hopefully, Ryan feels the same way. I'll know soon enough, by how he responds to my answer: "He claims he'll release Jack if I...that is, if I become a Quorum operative."

"Oh? And did you agree?" Ryan frowns, but his finger stays off the trigger of the gun in his hand.

I hesitate because telling Ryan shows just how far I'll go to get my husband back where he belongs: home, in my arms.

It may also earn me a bullet between the eyes.

Finally, I nod.

To my relief, he places his gun on the table. "You did the right thing." He grins. "I've always wanted someone on the inside."

"I was hoping you'd say that." I sink further into my chair. "Seriously, Ryan, do you think it's possible for me to fool Eric?"

"You can, and you will—and you'll do it with Acme's help. But we should keep your triple-agent status on a need-to-know basis."

"Agreed. Arnie, of course. And Emma. Abu too."

He nods. "They'll be your shadows and provide any necessary intercepts. I'm adding Dominic to the team too." Noting my wince, he adds, "Trust me, he has his own reasons for seeing Eric fail."

"If you say so." I shrug. "In any regard, it won't be easy. Eric promised to put me through some tests, whatever that means."

"It means that Acme has to figure out how to

neutralize the results of your successes. As long as we're kept abreast of your next mission, we'll be able to stay one step ahead of you. That way, we can tweak the outcomes so that they satisfy Eric, but ward off an international incident. Speaking of which"—he hesitates, then adds—"are you okay with keeping POTUS in the loop as well?"

His question stops me cold. "I...I really hadn't thought of it. If you're asking me if I trust Lee, the answer is yes." On the other hand, up until yesterday, Jack has always had doubts about Lee Chiffray. This is one way in which Lee can prove him wrong, once and for all. Ryan and I both know this.

Ryan nods. "I feel the same way. And now that both Eileen and Frannie are no longer part of the equation, I don't think we have to worry that the White House is still compromised."

"As far as I'm concerned, Babette is still a wildcard," I insist. "She's always in the wrong place at the wrong time, and with the wrong people. Tell him sorry, but Babette does not make the cut."

"I read you loud and clear. Jack's life is at stake. I'd get Lee's full understanding that no one other than you, he, and my Acme mission team must know." Ryan shakes his head. "On another note: I presume you don't have a pair of surveillance contact lenses on you, or your audio earbuds."

"Nope," I say with a snort. "I didn't feel it necessary to transmit what was supposed to be my honeymoon night to Acme headquarters."

A sad smile rises on his lips. "I'll put your shadows in place immediately. One will intercept you with whatever toys you'll need to subvert Eric's agenda. To that end, I think I should give you this now."

He goes to the brick wall surrounding the fireplace. He places his hand on one of the bricks—it's high, to the right. As he presses, it springs out into his palm. With his other hand, he reaches deep into the now empty space—

And pulls out something. "What is that, a survival tin?" I ask.

"You could say that." He motions me forward. "Do you know what happened to Acme's last agency director?"

I shake my head. "I presumed retirement."

"Something like that—but earlier than expected, and not by choice. He was kidnapped and tortured, along with his wife and children. We found them too late. His family didn't make it. He was barely alive." Ryan shrugs. "Their deaths put him over the edge. He put a gun in his mouth, so I guess you could say his torturers killed him too."

"I'm sorry to hear that, Ryan."

"He wasn't the first to be kidnapped, and he won't be the last." Ryan opens the tin and pulls out a tiny velvet pouch. Two things fall into his open palm. He holds up one of them: a miniscule see-through microchip, cylindrical in shape and no bigger than a grain of rice. "Since then, DARPA—the Defense Advanced Research Projects

Agency—has come up with a prototype for a subcutaneous tracking chip."

"You mean, some sort of GPS tracker, injected under the skin?"

"Affirmative. Directors of black-ops organizations with high security rankings were asked to be beta-testers, for obvious reasons."

I nod. "You're desirable kidnap targets."

"And for even more obvious reasons, most of us balked at the honor." He shrugs. "I guess what happened to Jack is reason enough to do so."

"I presume it's not battery-operated. Otherwise it would be too big to inject under the skin, not to mention a potential biohazard to the wearer."

"Right again. In fact, it's operated by a bio fuel cell. Glucose from your bloodstream gives it enough energy to emit the GPS signal strong enough to be tracked by satellite."

He takes the other item in his right hand: an EpiPen. "If you're game, I'll inject it in you. That way, we'll always have eyes on you—just in case…well—"

"In case I go missing." I sigh. "I understand. Okay, well, let's do this thing. Any suggestion as to where?"

"Ideally, your lower thigh."

"Yowch. Well, I guess it will have to do, until we've got something like James Bond's 'smart blood'." I lift my leg onto a chair but turn my head. No need to watch.

He lifts my yoga pants high enough that he can prick me in the back of my thigh, above the bend of my knee.

It doesn't hurt, but instinctively, I flinch anyway.

"They're watching our room. I'd better get back to the hotel." I rub the sting from the spot before lowering my pant leg again. Hesitantly, I add, "Ryan, I'll be honest: I didn't know exactly how you'd react to my news, but I was praying that we'd be of like minds regarding this problem. Thank you for understanding. You've been like a father to Jack—to both of us, really."

"I love Jack too, Donna. The goal is to bring him home, safe and sound." His smile curdles into his trademark grimace. "But it won't be easy. Compromises will be made. Here's hoping they're all ones we can live with."

I bow my head. "Is it too forward of me to ask you about Natalie?"

Slowly he nods. "Thank you for caring enough to do so. My wife never really knew what I did for a living—at least, not until the day she died."

"You kept it from her, the way Carl kept it from me."

He nods. "An Acme corporate mandate, set up by my predecessor, for obvious reasons. Personally, I rue the day I broke the news to her."

I have to ask: "Why?"

"I'd like to think she'd still be alive today." He shakes his head. "Then again, maybe I'm fooling myself."

"What happened?"

"I came home late that night. I'd never seen her so happy. She told me she was pregnant." He smiles at the memory. "To celebrate, we made love. And in the throes of passion, I told her everything: what I really did for a living, how I was recruited, and the number of missions I'd had to that point—even the fact that I was a hard man."

"I guess she didn't take it well?"

His smile dissolves into sadness. "That's putting it mildly! I couldn't stand the thought that she and our child would never know this side of me. Instead, the realization that I'd lied about my profession in the four years we'd been together was abhorrent to her. Then when she heard about my exterminations, she recoiled. She declared she'd married a monster." He shrugs. "Maybe she was right. To do what we do doesn't exactly make us good people—or ideal spouses for that matter."

I lift my head. "Our job is to save lives, even if it means taking a few."

"That wasn't exactly the reaction you had when I told you what Carl did for a living."

I shrug. "Like Natalie, I felt deceived. But did I think of Carl as a monster? Not then, anyway. Only when I discovered how he duped you and Acme, and that he did it for money and power, did I feel as if his sacrifice—and mine—had been for nothing. It was only at that point that I hated him." I take Ryan's hand in mine. "Perhaps it was when and how you broke the news to her that caused her to react in that manner. Coupled with all she was feeling about the baby, of course it would have been devastating news." I hesitate, then ask: "Did you offer to resign?"

He looks up at me. "It was her one condition, but I said no. That's how big of an asshole I am." He shakes his head. "Donna, I just couldn't bring myself to do it! I thought she'd eventually see the importance of our mission, and that things would work themselves out." He purses his lips. "No, to be honest with you, I was stubborn. I'm not the greatest communicator, you already know that."

He's right, but I'm not about to kick a good man when he's down.

"On the evening it happened, she ran out of the house. I followed her out and ran after her. That night it was storming. All winter long, Los Angeles had been experiencing torrential rainstorms." He falls into a chair. "I cornered her out there, in the back on the hill, but she refused to come back into the house with me. She said the last thing she wanted was to raise a child with a monster. She vowed I'd never come near them. I was so angry that I reached up to slap her. She took a step backward. Her feet slipped out from under her. I reached for her, but it was too late. She tumbled over the cliff." His eyes shut, as if the memory still lays heavy on his mind. "The rescue squad found her the next day. Her neck was broken." He buries his head in his hands. "I killed her."

"No, Ryan! You can't blame yourself."

"I did, and I always will." He shakes his head adamantly. "If I had it to do all over again, I would have put my family first. In life, it's the only thing that counts. Please, never forget that." He takes enough control of his emotions to look up at me. "My only solace is that I do my job to the best of my ability. Otherwise, her death—and the death of our child—is meaningless."

Words elude me. All I can do is put my hand on his shoulder.

In time, he gets ahold of himself. He lumbers out of the chair to the door. "You'd better get going."

He's right. Time is of the essence. I kiss the top of his head before heading out the door.

3

Separation Anxiety

When you were a'courtin', it seemed as if you were joined at the hip. Needless to say, you presumed the vow, "I do," also meant a twenty-four hour lovefest, just the two of you. But now that he's put a ring on your finger, you find him acting more distant —

If you find him at all. Why, the li'l booger seems to have taken off to parts unknown!

Not to worry — that is, if you planted a Global Positioning System bug on his cellphone…

Ooops! Looks like he realized that it was in his cellphone, which he left at home.

What, you say you also sewed another tracker in the hem of his jacket? Well, good for you for having such forethought…

Until you notice he left the jacket behind, too.

Oh, dear.

Eventually, he will come home to you.

And you will forgive him.

But you will never forget the time he got away.

So, after your "miss-you sex," when he's fast asleep, there's one more thing you can do: slap on a GPS ankle monitor.

Granted, doing so will certainly let the cat out of the bag regarding your need to keep tabs on him. Still, look on the bright side: besides the fact that he'll have to saw off his foot to keep you at bay, it proves to him how far you'll go to stay by his side.

DAMN, DAMN, DAMN HIGHWAY ONE TRAFFIC! EVEN AT THIS early morning hour—even going against traffic—my quest to find Ryan took me over two hours, round trip.

I've been away for much too long to be sobbing my heart out in the shower.

Since leaving him, I've kept one eye on the road, and the other on my phone's screen. It displays the security feed of my hotel, switching back between the parking lot and my suite's front door.

Now that I'm only three blocks from the hotel, I should be breathing easy—

But something on my cell screen catches my eye: a stretch limousine has just pulled up to the hotel's back parking lot. The driver hops out in order to open the door for the person in the back seat:

Eric Webber.

Shit.

Okay, I've got to move fast.

I hit the gas so that I take the last four blocks at warp speed. Suddenly I hear the yelp of a police siren. The officer flashes his lights to let me know that he's on my tail.

I can't stop for obvious reasons: first, it's not my car; second, I'm driving without my license; and third, I've got to be in that room when Eric knocks on the door.

All the more reason to outrun the police car.

I turn right, down a residential street—

And flick off my lights—

Before veering into a driveway with an open garage. I'm far enough away from him that he drives right by it, and on up into one of Laguna's hills.

I hear a loud meow beneath the car. Oh, my God, I could have run over a cat!

Quickly, I get out of the car, and crouch down beside it. The cat's golden eyes glow when caught in my cell-phone's flashlight. Her fur is black.

She's angry enough to spring at me, claws bared.

In the nick of time, I dodge out of the way.

She takes off into the night.

I wonder if I'm cursed. For Jack's sake, I hope not.

My heart is beating so fast that I have to sit for a moment and take deep breaths—a good thing, too, since the police car must have circled around, because now it's heading my way.

I watch as he turns back onto Highway One. Thank goodness he's heading in the opposite direction of the hotel.

I roll the Lexus out of the garage. A moment later, I've parked it back where I found it—a block from the hotel—and I hightail it back to my hotel.

ERIC AND ONE OF HIS OPERATIVES ARE NOW GETTING INTO the elevator.

Needless to say, I'll take the stairs.

I use the housekeeper's key to get me into the hotel's back door, and into the emergency exit staircase, which I take to the roof, where I'll climb down onto the terrace of my hotel suite—

Except for the fact that there's a bald hulking block of a man on the balcony beside mine, smoking a cigarette. His feet sit in a circle of dead butts.

Is he another one of Eric's operatives?

I get my answer when I hear Eric shout, "Gunter!" The man answers, "*Ja, kommt!*" as he heads back inside.

I slide down the rain pipe onto my terrace, and leap through the sliding door to my bedroom. I tear off my clothes before jumping into the bathroom shower.

The water is tepid at best. I'm sure the rest of the hotel's guests won't appreciate the hot water hog.

In no time at all, I'm soaked.

I slip into one of the hotel's complimentary terry robes.

As I wrap a towel around my damp hair, I take a quick glance at myself in the mirror. My mascara is smeared around my eyes, as if I've been crying for the past few hours.

Good. Let Eric presume that I'm devastated.

That I'm weak, and I'll do anything he wants.

In other words, I'll have him right where I want him.

"WE AREN'T DISTURBING YOU, ARE WE, MY DARLING MRS. Craig?" Eric has thought nothing of letting himself and three of his colleagues into my suite. His voice greets me from the bed, where my honeymoon bliss had just taken place.

On the bed I should now be sleeping in, with Jack.

I don't recognize two of the other men. One is small, wiry and non-descript. He smirks as if he thinks he's got something on me. The other is a tall square-jawed hunk with pale blue eyes separated by a lazy auburn forelock. He turns toward me and leers, as if we share a secret.

The third man is Gunter. He is going through my suitcase when something catches his eye: one of my negligees. I don't like his leer as he scrutinizes its sheerness. Carelessly, he stretches it, as if testing its strength—as what, a restraint? If so, it fails, as it rips into two pieces.

The lout tosses it over his shoulder as if it's some rag. It drifts to the floor, like the promise of a dream that is never to come true.

We'll see about that.

As Eric rises, he straightens imaginary wrinkles from his medium gray Brioni suit. He then has the audacity to finger a wet tendril that has escaped my towel turban. I steel myself from flinching.

Instead, I nod toward the living room. "The sooner we talk business, the sooner I get my husband back—that is, if you're good to your word. I'll be with you shortly."

"Ah, well, you see, Mrs. Craig, I plan on keeping you in sight at all times." He nods toward his colleagues. "A necessary evil."

I frown. "Don't be ridiculous. If I'm to accomplish my tasks, I can't have any of your goons tagging along."

Eric's harsh laugh reveals teeth as white as his shoulder-length mane. "My colleagues are the very soul of discretion. You won't even know they are there."

I scoop up the torn negligee off the floor. "Yeah, okay, if you say so. But your mutts stay out of my way, unless I whistle for them." I toss it in Gunter's face.

He's angry enough to take a step in my direction.

I can dig it. Still, no better time than now to put this relationship in perspective, right?

I grab his nutsack and twist as hard as I can. Gunter howls loudly and indignantly, before crumpling to the floor.

Weasel's eyes narrow. Apparently, he takes Gunter's whimpers as a rallying cry. As he charges me, a switchblade opens in his right hand, but it slices the air when I deke left. Before he's had time to turn and parry, I've reached for my perfume spray bottle on the dresser. A generous spritz of *Dior Pure Poison* has him screaming and clawing at his eyes.

I know one way to shut his yap: jab him in the throat.

He keels over, gasping for air.

I curl a finger in Pretty Boy's direction. He throws up his hands, its fingertips facing me. "New polish. Don't want to muss it." He purses his lips to make his point.

Been there, done that.

I lift Weasel's knife from the floor. I then pull Gunter's gun—a Glock 21—from his back holster. I smile pretty at Eric. "You know what they say: finders, keepers."

Eric roars with laughter. "Now that you've established a pecking order, Mrs. Craig, I'll do the honor of a much belated introduction to your entourage." He nods toward the human weasel. "This is Hugo Kaspar. He underestimated you. But despite his diminutive physique, I would caution you about doing the same to him." Next, Eric points to Pretty Boy. "Varick Velasco will accompany you on some of your more formal social outings. Don't be fooled by his vanity, or his *bon vivant* demeanor. He won't hesitate to kill you if you attempt to sully my goals."

Varick's wolfish leer goes flat and his eyes deaden into dark slits. A shiver charges up my spine.

Eric waves in the direction of Gunter, who has finally stopped writhing on the floor. "I'm sorry that Gunter overstepped your boundaries. I promise, should he do so again, it will be at my command only." When his eyes shift to me, the smile is now a steely grimace.

"Good to know." I shrug. "In the meantime, let's get one thing straight. Since this isn't a peepshow, only one of you can stay while I dress. For all I care, you can toss a coin for the honor."

Eric smiles at my flippancy. But from the way he flicks his hand at the others, he proves being the boss has its benefits. "Wait in the next room."

Hugo glowers as he storms off. Gunter limps out of the room as fast as he possibly can. Varick's disappointment is declared in a sad sigh as he follows them out.

I wait until the door shuts before disrobing.

I won't look at Eric. I don't need to, as I feel his eyes on me.

And I hear his footsteps coming toward me. He moves in so close that I feel his breath on the back of my neck. "Turn around," he commands me.

I do so, slowly.

Eric has knelt in front of me. Like I said, it's a peepshow—only up close and personal.

Slowly and methodically, his hands follow the contours of my naked body, hovering mere inches from my skin. He wets his lips with the tip of his tongue. Should I be worried that there is desire in his eyes? Wouldn't it be worse for me—for Jack—if there were none?

Since Jack, I've kept my honeypot days to a minimum. That's not to say that I haven't had my fair share of slaps and tickles, but the hanky-panky stopped before the point of no return—for me, anyway.

As for my targets, if I didn't turn them or apprehend them, I killed them.

In regard to Eric, the first two alternatives aren't going to happen. The third creates an undesirable conundrum, since I need to play him as long as possible.

Decisions, decisions. What should I do if he licks, bites, or penetrates me? Do I just stand here and take it?

Hell no, that's not part of our deal.

I could lift a knee straight up into his chin and knock him out cold. With a quick twist of my wrists, I could break his neck—

But then I'd lose Jack forever.

So I keep my cool and stay as still as a statue.

I look down to see him staring at the tiny puncture on the back of my left thigh. When he moves his index finger toward it, I steel myself from flinching.

He stops himself from touching it.

Instead, he kisses it.

Finally, Eric murmurs, "Exquisite, even with the mosquito bite. But despite all temptations, one must not mix business with pleasure." He rises again in order to saunter back to the bed, and lowers himself on it, as if he owns it. When he nods, I head for the closet.

I try not to shiver at the thought of him scrutinizing me from behind.

Instead, I pull out a pair of sleek black leather slacks with one hand, and a sheer white silk blouse with the other.

Eric shrugs. "That will do for the flight to your next

destination, but not for the mission. For that, you'll need something a bit more…shall we say, seductive?"

"Perhaps if you explained the task at hand, I could pack accordingly."

"Nothing too complicated, my dear. You're to attend a cocktail party at the Russian consulate in San Francisco. There, you'll rendezvous with a dear old friend of mine, and hand him this." He puts a thumb drive in my palm, then closes my hand over it. For a moment, his hand lingers there as he strokes my knuckles.

"What is it exactly?"

"Are you sure you want to know?"

"If I'm going down for treason, I should at least know why."

He laughs uproariously. "It'll be a cakewalk! No need to worry your pretty little head."

"Who is my contact?" I ask.

"His name is Konstantin Sumarokov. He is a deputy trade representative." He looks at his watch. "I'll tell you more on the way to the airport."

I didn't like the set-up for several reasons. First, handing off anything of national importance to a Russian intelligence agent would make me a traitor. And secondly, the consulate's video surveillance would be sure to document my deed—if not to convict me, then to blackmail me at a later date.

But there's nothing I can do about it except to get dressed.

And perhaps satisfy Eric's question as to my loyalty, at least enough that he'd let his guard down.

He's in for a real show. I pluck a gold lamé gown from the closet, and hold it in front of me. "Will this do?"

Eric gives his approval with a sly smile.

I lay it on the bed beside him. He strokes the gown's bodice, as if imagining me in it. When I bought it, I imagined Jack doing the same, with a similar look of longing in his eyes.

I saunter to the dresser, where I pull out a nude thong panty. I hold it up to admire before letting my gaze fall on Eric. He nods.

He watches as I slip into it. Next, I pull out a matching push-up bra. I position it over my breasts, but when I reach around to fix the clasp, he is standing behind me. "Let me help you with that."

I stop.

He takes this as my tacit approval.

As he hooks the clasp, his fingers brush against my back.

I resist the urge to ram my fist into his neck and crush his esophagus.

I'll save that thrill for when I know Jack is safe.

Just one of the many things we do for love.

4

Jack's Diary, Day 1

DONNA…

Ah, hell, my head is killing me.

Keep it together, Jack. Focus.

Just…

Focus.

Okay, here goes:

Donna, my love, I don't know how long I've been out of it, but I presume by now you've figured out I'm gone.

I know you well enough to realize you'll do everything in your power to find out how it happened, and, eventually, where they've taken me.

In the meantime, I'll do my best to escape, or at least to stay alive until we're together again.

Because, yes, I swear to you: I won't die this way.

In the meantime, for my own sanity, I'm making a

mental diary of everything that happens to me. As we both know all too well, every little detail comes in handy.

I'll also leave a trail of breadcrumbs. So far, it isn't ideal: my blood on a button from a head wound—but, thankfully, not from a bullet.

By now, my guess is that Arnie has pulled the hotel's security video, and Acme knows my abductors were a woman playing housekeeper, as well as some guy acting as her muscle. You'll also see that they towed me away in a laundry bin.

Sadly, I drifted off before I could hear or see anything that might give you an idea as to which direction we're headed.

Shit, I wonder how long I've been out?

I have no sensory perception, either, because my mouth is gagged, I'm blindfolded, and I'm hogtied in some kind of padded box.

Mariachi music plays on the radio, which means we're still in California, or perhaps Arizona.

Or else we've crossed the border into Mexico—

Oh…

Fuck.

MY HEAD SLAMS AGAINST THE TOP OF MY COFFIN. I MUST have fallen asleep again, but the road is so bumpy now that my bones seem to rattle in my skin.

It must be daylight because this box is a hellish

inferno.

"*Ay, Dios mio!*" Someone yells. Translation: Oh, my God.

It sounds as if he's right beside me.

Another voice answers him: "Shut up, Pedro! This *culero* will kill you for sneezing, let alone for talking."

Belligerently, Pedro retorts, "*¡Me vale madres!*"

"*Si, hombre,*" the other man hisses, "You certainly will 'give a fuck' when he comes in here and blasts us to Kingdom Come!" He sighs. "Why did I listen to you? Robbing from El Maestro—*what was I thinking?*"

"You were thinking of your mother's operation, and your little brother's future should he stay in the poppy fields, and of your pregnant girlfriend! If we hadn't gotten caught, we could have gotten them out of Paraíso, and eventually over the border—"

"But we did get caught! My God, Pedro! Do you know what El Maestro will do to us? My mother and my brother and my girlfriend will see my head hanging from a post in the plaza!" He kicks the side of my box. "See these boxes? Do you know what they keep in here? They are not the dead, amigo! They are *los condenados*—the condemned! They are going to El Maestro's hellhole—and so are we." Pedro's friend sobs uncontrollably.

The driver must have heard him too, because the van rolls to a complete stop.

Both men stop talking. It's almost as if they've stopped breathing.

We can all hear it: the engine stops. The driver lets

loose with a long sigh. Finally, the door on the driver's side opens.

Pedro's friend whimpers through the Lord's Prayer in Spanish.

Heavy footsteps make their way to the back of the van. The click of metal—like a key finding its niche in a lock.

"*¡Cállate!*" Pedro hisses. His friend does what he says: he shuts up.

The creak of hinges on a metal door as it opens. The van drops an inch as someone steps in.

Silence.

"Who's the loudmouth?" the driver growls.

Neither man says anything.

"Speak up, or I'll shoot you both."

Again, silence. Then Pedro's friend whimpers, "*No, no no…!*"

A shot goes off.

Footsteps move toward the door. There's a thump as they hit the pavement. The door slams shut. The lock clicks into place.

I smell shit. Pedro must have shit his pants, or the body of his dead friend has evacuated itself.

Or else it was one of the other condemned who are locked in a box like me.

This El Maestro guy must be a drug lord who does business with the Quorum.

If so, you may never find me, Donna.

I'll have to find my way back to you.

I will, I promise, darling, no matter what.

5

Kiss and Make Up

Dear wives, the first rule of marriage is, simply this: never go to bed angry.

Granted, there will be times in which you feel as if Hubby is being pig-headed and unreasonable, and that nothing you say will change his mind.

You're probably right.

Still, 'tis no reason to pout the night away. Instead, remember this axiom:

Actions speak louder than words.

And speaking of axioms and actions, no better time to also remember that nicely sharpened axe in the woodshed. One swing and (preferably) a miss, and he'll be ready to talk turkey! In fact, he'll probably be jabbering his head off, begging you to "remember how much we love each other," and how he didn't mean what he said, that he was just teasing, and to remind you how bad it looks to the cops when you go off half-cocked—

Which will jog your memory as to the gun you hide in your unmentionables drawer.

Pointed at a certain appendage, at that point you can ask, "Oh, yeah? Now what's half-cocked?"

No doubt it'll be an answer you both agree on, and therefore no need to go to bed angry.

ERIC IS ACCOMPANYING US IN THE LIMO TO JOHN WAYNE International Airport, but he insists he will not be joining us on this mission. "Varick will be at your side. Gunter will shadow you as well," he assures me with a pat on my hand.

Gunter's acknowledgement of this is a grunt, whereas Varick honors me with a seductive smirk.

Eric hands me a United Airlines ticket booked for SFO.

"Not a private jet?" I can't help but laugh. "And I'm to fly coach at that! I was under the impression that the Quorum spared no expense for its operatives."

Eric shrugs. "I'll need the jet later today. When you're done with your mission, you and the others will once again rendezvous with me." He opens the valise that was handed to him by Hugo when he entered the limo. Inside are glasses, a blond wig, and a wallet. "Wear these as you go through TSA. Familiarize yourself with your new identity."

I open the wallet to find a driver's license. It tells me that I'm Mona Henshaw from San Jose, California.

"Mona is attending the reception at the Russian Consulate. When you get there, you can skip the glasses." Eric shrugs. "We want all the boys to make passes, now don't we?"

I frown. "You tell me."

"Just one in particular." He pulls a photo from his inside breast pocket. It is of a man: broad-shouldered and quite handsome, in his mid-thirties. However, his face has an ugly scar on one cheek. "There will be a string quartet playing Russian classics. A man by the name of Konstanin Sumarokov will ask you to dance a waltz. Of course you'll say yes. Somehow, you'll end up in an alcove with him, all the better to take in an incomparable view of the Golden Gate Bridge."

"Sounds scrumptious."

"Remember, Mrs. Craig, these things can turn deadly if you don't take them seriously."

"I told you, I'll do anything to get Jack back, alive and well."

"Then you'll hand off the thumb drive to Konstantin. Once he ascertains that the data is real, you'll be allowed to leave with your escorts." Eric nods toward Varick and Gunter.

I pull the memory stick from the outside pocket of my valise and hold it up to him. "How will your pal know it's legitimate?"

"He may not, but being a scientist, he knows the

encryption code that opens the file, my pet." He shakes out the wig and tosses it into my lap.

"If it isn't the right code, will I be allowed to leave anyway?" I ask.

"Unfortunately, no." He shakes his head in mock mournfulness. "It's a chance you'll have to take."

"Why me? Why not one of your goons here?" I lean back against the seat. "For that matter, why not you?"

"In the world of espionage, I am God. And like God, I may not be seen, but my presence is felt everywhere." He waves a hand in Varick's direction. "As for your entourage, neither of them can carry off gold lamé, although I'd bet Varick would be willing to try."

Varick shakes his head vigorously. "Not really. Gold is the only shade that does nothing for my skin tone."

"You'd have better luck if you stayed out of the tanning booth," I mutter. Still, my grimace is for Eric. "For that matter, how do I know you aren't just setting me up as a traitor, so that I end up in jail, and Jack gets killed anyway?"

"A set-up? What would be the fun in that? Donna, let me make something perfectly clear. I *want* you to succeed." Eric smiles broadly. "And something tells me you'll enjoy these little tests as much as I do."

He may be right—not that I'd let him know it. "Eric, we have a deal: four trials, then I get Jack: safe, sound, and in one piece."

His ghoulish grin fades. "Mrs. Craig, if I'm nothing else, I'm a man of my word."

We shall see.

I put the thumb drive back in the valise pocket. At the same time, I pull out a mirror. I look at my reflection as I position the wig on my head.

Varick obviously thinks that "Mona Henshaw" is quite a looker because he he licks his lips.

I honor him with a middle-finger salute. Just keepin' it real.

THE TSA SECURITY LINE SNAKES THROUGH A QUEUE THAT eventually breaks into six smaller lines, each with its own scanning machine. Gunter is in front of me, Varick is behind me. Both were smart enough to allow other passengers to get in between us.

I don't notice until I'm asked for my driver's license by the guard at the first station that I recognize his voice:

Abu.

He frowns as he scrutinizes Mona's license, then in a low voice murmurs, "Does the rug match the drapes?"

I have to purse my lips to keep from guffawing.

Loudly, he proclaims, "Take the line on the far left."

I put away my license and head over in the direction he pointed.

Arnie is working the scanner.

I look ahead. Gunter was sent to the far right. Dominic is standing beside the line's body scanner. He has darkened his hair, and wears glasses, along with a Fu Manchu mustache. I pray he doesn't attempt an American accent. Even a Teutonic cretin like Gunter might spot it as a fake.

As Gunter enters the machine, it beeps loudly. Gunter looks up, startled. He scowls as Dominic runs the security baton over him and it beeps again.

By the time I reach Arnie, Dominic has ushered Gunter into a small room, and shut the door behind them.

A strip search? That ought to be fun.

By now, Abu has put Varick in the scanner line with the longest queue of all. One of the guards working it is Emma. Varick seems to be panicking. I guess he thinks I'll bolt.

Hardly. I'm having too much fun watching my team at play.

I PUT THE THUMB DRIVE IN THE SECURITY TRAY ALONG WITH my cellphone.

Arnie yawns, then picks it up. How can I get word to him that it's intel vital to national security?

Almost as if reading my mind, Arnie's nod is imperceptible. He also motions me through the scanner. I walk through slowly, to give him the time he needs to do whatever voodoo that he does so well.

Even as I leave the body scanner, my valise is rolling off the X-ray machine, along with the security tray with my cellphone.

The thumb drive is gone.

The second I pick up my phone, it buzzes with a text.

I glance around before answering. Gunter is stuck in TSA purgatory, while Varick is waiting behind another four people before he gets his chance at the body scanner. Angrily, he tosses his pair of very expensive John Lobb brogues in a security bin.

Just sitting down on one of the benches beyond the security area gives me the coverage I need to read the text:

Bugged E's limo, and his goon's room and yours, so know your destination as well as contents of the drive. Need time to break encryption, scan, and hand off a dupe. Will do it on plane. Later baby! PS: This message self-destructs in 3...2...

What a nut.

I look up just as Varick is coming out of the body scanner. I wave him over as if we're old pals.

He is not amused.

What, can't take a joke? Too bad.

In case someone is watching, he walks just beyond me, but he's still close enough to hear my taunt, "What took you so long?"

He's about to snap at me when we both notice Gunter rushing from the security safe room. He looks as if he's going to bust a gut, he's so angry. He's sputtering what I presume to be German cuss words.

Varick walks just past him, and cuts him short with a steely stare. "Let's get to our gate, shall we?" he hisses.

He takes off first. I examine my lips in my compact, as

if I have all the time in the world. I wait until he's some thirty feet in front of me before following.

Gunter is grabbing his suitcase, which has been waiting for him at the end of the TSA station's conveyor belt.

By now, I'm sure a tracker has been sewn into it.

If I had my way, it would be a bomb that went off when I pushed the detonator once I'm far away from the cretin. I'll see what Arnie can do about that.

Varick and Gunter have aisle seats: Varick's is in front by an aisle, whereas Gunter sits in the row opposite mine, where I've taken the window seat.

Gunter must be dying for a cigarette. He smacks his mouthful of nicotine gum so loudly that his seatmates are giving him evil looks.

My seat partners are a twenty-something couple with an adorable baby: Emma and Arnie.

Their disguises are so good—an auburn-haired wig and bushy beard for him, glasses and a fun bun for her— that even I would not have recognized them except for the toddler in their arms: their son, Nicky.

Apparently, he recognizes me too because he gives out a squeal and a laugh. But before he can call out his name for me—"Dahnahnahnah"—Emma puts a pacifier in his mouth.

Arnie takes his time shoving his family's bags into the

overhead compartment, so that he can give Emma the coverage needed to whisper, "We had a hell of a time finding a thumb drive that matched the one Eric gave you. The moment we reach cruising altitude, we'll try to crack it and see what's up. If so, we can give you a dupe with muddied intel."

I nod ever so slightly. "Where was Nicky when you were undercover?"

"Ryan was keeping an eye on him, in the TSA employee lounge."

This truly is a family affair—my office family, that is.

Suddenly, I miss my children. Heck, I even miss Aunt Phyllis. It seems a million years ago since I held any of them in my arms, or heard their laughter.

I imagine Jack is thinking the same thing.

So that Emma can't see the sadness in my face, I open the airline magazine and feign interest in an article about fly-fishing on the Rogue River.

It looks beautiful. Maybe Jack and I will go up to Oregon sometime.

I tear up at the thought that I may never see him again.

I wipe away the dampness on my face and just in time: Varick, annoyed that Arnie is blocking his view, stands up so that he can look over the seats in order to see what I'm up to.

I smile up at him, as if I don't have a care in the world. It's the only way I'll survive this living hell.

THE MOMENT WE REACH CRUISING ALTITUDE, EMMA LOWERS her seat table and places soft toys on it for Nicky's amusement. At the same time, under the table she passes me a couple of pair of surveillance contact lenses, as well as some audio earrings.

Arnie has already put the thumb drive into his computer, and is running it through an encryption program.

With each minute that passes, I'm chewing my nails down to the quick.

When Gunter glances over, invariably his eyes fall on Arnie's screen. From his point of view, what he sees is a hologram of a replay of a Lakers basketball game. It's appropriate, considering the grunts and curses Arnie gives as we wait for program to run its course.

Finally, Arnie crows, "Boo-YAH!"

The other passengers turn, annoyed or curious—including Gunter and Varick.

The scary sound from his daddy causes Nicky to wail. "Henry, please! The baby," Emma scolds him with a punch to the arm. "It's only a basketball game!"

Arnie nods meekly, even as he downloads the encrypted file onto his computer. When he realizes what he's looking at, he lets loose with a low whistle and mutters, "We can't turn this stuff over to the bad guys! It contains the coordinates for the secret undersea fiber-optic cable that carries all broadband communications between our government's defense department and its EU counterparts!"

"I can see why it's so important to the Russians," I murmur. "There are close to a thousand cables crossing under our oceans. Knowing the right cable will allow them to monitor it via a wiretap."

Emma nods. "They want tit for tat. We've done the same to them."

"Worse yet, when they finally hear something they don't like"—Arnie scissors the air with the index and middle fingers of both hands—"Snip, snip!"

"What can we do to muddy this intel?" I ask.

Emma shrugs. "Change a coordinate or two…or three."

"Hmmm…" Arnie stares hard at the screen. "Do you think they'd believe we'd route such an important cable to the exact site where they found the Titanic?"

"Who knows? I say go for it," I whisper. "And hurry! This is a short flight. Any moment now, the pilot will start his descent into San Francisco."

I look out the window. It's already getting dark. There is enough light emanating from the inside of the plane's cabin to catch Arnie's reflection as he jiggers with the diagram's coordinates before downloading it on the second thumb drive.

A few minutes later, he declares, "Touchdown!"

"You're supposed to be watching a basketball game," Emma reminds him.

He shrugs. "Tomato, to-*mah*-toe."

"Silly man." She tweaks his nose.

He kisses her cheek.

I look down at my hands, not because I'm embarrassed for catching them at this intimate moment, but because I'm missing Jack so much. I wish he were here to kiss me.

At that very moment, Nicky goes boom boom in his diaper.

In unison, the noses of those in the seats in front, beside, and behind us wrinkle up as they sniff the air.

Even Varick can smell it. He rises up and looks at me, as if I'm the culprit. When Varick sees Emma and Arnie trading Nicky and the diaper bag for the computer, his eyes roll skyward. It's enough to make him sit back down.

In a flash, I've slipped on the contact lenses and my earbud. "Hello, gorgeous," Ryan murmurs in my ear.

All my angels are watching over me.

Soon they will be watching over you too, Jack, I vow silently.

As Arnie heads down the aisle toward the lavatory, Emma murmurs, "Dominic will be shadowing you at the party. Abu is following Eric."

I squeeze her hand to say thanks.

She opens a magazine and holds it up to her face so that Gunter can't see us talking. "Has Eric given you any clues as to where he's stashing Jack?"

"No. And even if I do everything he asks, there's certainly no guarantee that he'll live up to his word to let Jack go free."

Emma frowns, but she keeps her eyes on the magazine. "What do you mean, 'everything'?"

"What? …Oh! No, not *that*!" I feel my face warming. "I meant successfully completing the missions he's lined up for me."

"Of course. I'm…sorry I inferred…the other." It's Emma's turn to blush. "Please don't worry, Donna. We'll do our best to stay one step ahead and stop whatever damage is caused. Just keep playing Eric—*no matter what it takes*." Her eyes shift from the page to my face to see if I catch her meaning. "Jack would never blame you if you… well, you know—had to do everything you could to win Eric's trust."

Just how far would I go to win Eric's trust in the hope of getting Jack back?

I don't know how to answer her.

I'm glad I don't have to, because the flight attendant's voice informs us that we're to stow our electronic equipment and put up our tray and seats because we're just minutes from being on the ground.

Arnie is chasing his toddler son down the aisle. Somehow, Nicky got hold of Arnie's fake beard.

Thank goodness, Arnie slaps it on just as Gunter looks up.

Right then and there, Emma remembers that she, Arnie, and Nicky aren't really on a family vacation. She pulls both the real thumb drive and the counterfeit one from the computer.

She hands me the counterfeit one as she scoops up her son and smothers him with kisses, while Arnie takes his seat beside her. "Close call," he mutters.

Something tells me this will be a week filled with close calls.

THE QUORUM HAS RENTED A SAFE HOUSE FOR THE EVENING, in which Varick, Gunter, and I dress prior to the Russian reception.

Gunter leaves an hour before Varick and me. Considering that his social skills don't go beyond grunts and smiles, I presume it's because he'll be part of the consulate's wait staff.

Closer to the witching hour, I slip into my gold lamé gown. I tuck the thumb drive into my matching clutch purse.

Varick and I share an Uber to the reception. The ride will be billed to an untraceable credit card. He asks the driver to drop him off two blocks from our final destination. That way, we reach the consulate separately. He looks smart in an Armani white tux. Despite being several yards away, his eyes never leave me. I still have to prove that I won't run.

He should know better than that. Jack's life depends on me being wherever Eric wants me.

I time my entrance to the Russian Consulate's gala to coincide with that of a large throng of other guests. The consulate is housed in an eight-story Edwardian brick mansion, located in San Francisco's crowning jewel neighborhood, Pacific Heights. Like Varick, the other men are in tuxedos, some studded with Russian Army chest candy. And like me, all the women are in sparkly gowns. Most of the guests are conversing in Russian, but I also hear English—with American twangs, British lilts, and Australian cheekiness—as well as a smattering of Spanish, French, and German.

Once the security guards check my identification at the massive double front doors, I join the line in which the Consul General and his wife receive their guests. A tall, broad man stands on the other side of the Consul General. He glances over sharply when he hears me say the name, "Mona Henshaw." From the way he looks me over, top to bottom, he apparently thinks he'll find pleasure in the business we have to conduct.

He'll be greatly disappointed. He won't hear why from me, but from his superiors, once they realize the intel on the thumb drive is bogus. By then, Jack should be safely home to me.

The mournful twang of a violin concerto summons the revelers into the grand ballroom beyond the reception hall. That's my cue to move on. I know my role well enough: Fit in and don't stand out. Let him make contact. Give him what he needs, then get out.

He doesn't keep me waiting long.

He does so by brushing his lips to my proffered hand, then declares, "So nice of you to make it here from Silicon Valley. My name is Konstantin Sumarokov. We welcome your company's interest in doing business with our country."

I dimple up. "It's an honor to be here."

I glance around in the hope that I see Dominic, but no luck. The place is jam-packed. Most of the attendees sit in chairs facing the string quartet, but others mill around the bars and food stations that are set up in strategic areas along the periphery of the ballroom.

The string quartet is playing a Stravinsky violin concerto when Konstantin Sumarokov's curt murmur warms my neck: "I wasn't told how beautiful you are."

I force my lips into a smile before turning to face him. "Flattery will get you a thumb drive—and nothing more."

He tosses his head back and laughs uproariously, as if I'd said something too clever by half. "How I love you American women! Madonnas or whores—no in between."

"Expect to genuflect," I warn him.

"A traitor to her country may one day need to seek asylum." His hand strokes my naked shoulder. "Our safe rooms are quite comfortable. Come and see for yourself."

Before I can say anything, his hand has found the small of my back in order to steer me up the circular staircase to the ballroom's upper loge.

His hand slips lower when we reach the top of the steps.

I catch Varick watching us. He shames me by blowing a kiss. I would love the honor of poking his eye out, if only to break him of this very annoying habit.

"Oh, my God, Donna! I'm so sorry! I handed you the wrong thumb drive!" The desperation in Emma's voice comes in through my earbud. "Brush pass with Dominic."

"Too late," I murmur.

"I beg your pardon?" Konstantin Sumarokov isn't really listening. He's too busy looking for an empty alcove. If the ones we've passed thus far aren't occupied with couples looking for privacy for some slap and tickle action, they hold frowning men whose hushed, fervent voices relay the status of other clandestine operations taking place here in enemy territory.

If only these walls had ears.

Who am I kidding? Of course they do. Which could mean that everything I say and do can be used against me in a U.S. court of law.

Oh…*hell.*

I shove his hand off my backside. "I said, let's get this over with."

He wrenches my arm behind my back in order to steer me into an empty alcove. "Eric warned me you might be a little feisty."

"He warned me too—that you might be"—I glance down below his beltline—"*little.*"

He slaps my face.

I have a knee-jerk reaction—

That is to say, my knee slams into his groin.

As he doubles over, I pick up my clutch purse.

Konstantin's way of announcing his desire that we kiss and make up is to draw his Glock. "Not so fast, Ms.

Henshaw. I don't want to 'shoot the messenger,' as they say."

Batting my lashes, I purr, "Aw, now, I don't want you to go off half-cocked." To make my point, I cup his crotch in my palm.

From what I can see, it has thickened instantly. He's all smiles again. "That's much better. Sometimes these transactions need a little finessing."

Just as he pulls me closer, we hear, "Champagne, as ordered!"

The accent is Russian, but this is not your typical waiter: Dominic. The tray in his left hand holds an uncorked champagne bottle and two crystal flutes. The napkin is folded over his right arm, which is folded over his waist.

Konstantin is as surprised as me. But before he can protest, I gush, "How thoughtful!" To emphasize my pleasure, I place my hand over his chest and squeeze his nipple between my index and middle fingers.

He's still grinning with anticipation when Dominic does his pratfall. The tray clatters onto the marble floor. The glasses shatter, and the bottle's contents drench the randy Russian.

Even as Dominic stutters profuse apologies and pats down Konstantin with the towel with one hand, he slaps the real duplicate thumb drive into my palm with the other.

I slip it into the plunging décolleté of my dress. I open

my clutch, grab the coveted thumb drive, and slip it into Dominic's tux pocket.

Slapping away Dominic's hand, Konstantin growls, "Get the hell out!"

Dominic stutters inanities as he bows his way out of the alcove.

"My, my, aren't we a mess!" I pick up where Dominic left off with the napkin, but by now it's sopping wet, and all I'm doing is ruining Konstantin's tux.

He realizes it too, and pushes my hand away.

I hold tight to his wrist. When he sees what I pull out from between my breasts—the duplicate thumb drive—he shrugs appreciatively.

I put it in his palm, closing his fingers over it.

Before he can say anything, I saunter out of the room.

He hasn't noticed that I've slipped his Glock into my clutch.

I'm sure it'll come in handy.

6

Jack's Diary, Day 2

Dear Donna,

The van has finally rumbled to a stop. Still, the engine is running.

It must be nightfall, because my box is much cooler.

The driver turns off the van's radio in order to greet someone—apparently a guard. I know this because he tells him, in Spanish: "Take the cargo to the basement." The driver knows guard well enough to call him by his first name—Tomás—and asks after the man's wife. He then makes a jab at Tomás's favorite soccer team, Club León, which must not be doing too well in the country's playoff games. In response, Tomás's growls, "*Chinga tu madre.*"

The driver laughs heartily as he revs the engine and heads on.

He takes a few turns before we lurch to a stop. He

opens his door and walks around to the back of the van. He's talking to someone. I can't make out his words, but the next thing I know the van door opens and a few men are shouting, "*¡Vamanos! ¡Vamanos!*"

I hear what must be some of the others in the van stumble to their feet. The van bounces as they jump out.

Next, I hear the scraping of heavy items being shoved forward toward the door—perhaps other boxes, like mine.

Then mine as well.

When my box hits the ground, I fly up, smacking my head against it. My grunt gives a sense of hilarity to those who open it: swarthy cruel-eyed men, muscular, but short.

A few have semi-automatic rifles slung around their shoulders. The rest have their guns pointed at the six men who have already been released. I presume one of these is Pedro, with dreams of escaping this prison known as Paraíso.

High bright lights blind me. When finally my eyes adjust, I see that we are in some sort of courtyard belonging to a three-story building. The yard's high walls are made of thick cinderblock, and topped with barbed wire. Guards with rifles laugh and shout from their open stations at the four corners of the yard.

The other six prisoners from the van have already been placed on their knees in front of swaybacked anvils. I'm also shoved down in front of one. A guard grabs me by my scalp and wrenches my head to the left, so that I am looking at the others.

A tall brawny man with a long-armed hatchet stands over the prisoner farthest from me. I hear the kneeling man pleading for his life. I recognize his voice: Pedro.

The blade's cut is swift, and silences him immediately.

His head rolls into the basket in front of the anvil.

By now, all the other prisoners are trembling. A few are babbling prayers. A second slice results in another thump in a straw basket.

Three more to go.

Is this how it ends for me?

To hell with that.

With all my might, I rise to my feet. My hands are still tied behind me, which is why the guard standing over me isn't prepared for my head butt to his gut. He topples to the ground.

Two more guards come at me. Before the first one can swing his rifle into position, I've kicked it out of his hands. My second kick hits him squarely in the jaw.

His head snaps back. When he falls, his head slams one of the now vacant anvils.

I am felled when one of the guards slams his rifle butt into my side. Another guard cracks me over the head with his sidearm.

I stumble to the ground. They grab me under my arms and drag me back to my anvil, slapping my head face down upon it. "*¡Oscar, aqui! Los demás pueden esperar. ¡Haga este culero primero!*"

I'm to be next.

So be it.

Donna, I pull your face into my mind's eye. How beautiful you looked on our wedding day, my darling! And how heartfelt was your vow to be my wife until death carried us apart.

Despite the fact that each day, our deadly occupation puts us at risk, I'd always presumed God would grant us a lifetime together.

I guess that was not meant to be.

The brute they call Oscar takes his place behind me. He waits until the heads of the few remaining prisoners are turned to watch my execution, when a man's voice calls out, *"¡Deténgase! Es que el Americano?"*

The guards quit laughing. They turn to the driver, who nods vigorously.

"¡Ay, Dios!" The man roars from the window. The barrage of Spanish that follows is much too fast for me to comprehend, but from what I can gather, my life has been spared.

But why? And for how long?

I'm left on the anvil to watch the executions of the others. The dead eyes in their heads seem to implore me —for what?

Afterward, the guards use my face as a punching bag. By the time I pass out, the blood from my broken nose is running into my mouth and I'm gagging.

Still, I'm alive.

~

An angel hovers over me.

I have felt her presence for some time now, soothing my wounds. One of my eyes refuses to open. The other sees her through a dark scrim of blood: a woman—a girl, really, as she can't be more than twenty. She wears a simple white shift. There is a tiny cross on the silver chain around her neck. A widow's peak of dark hair can be seen through the white scarf on her head.

As long as I can see her gentle smile, I know there is still a God.

When the haze of pain lifts, I can finally see my surroundings: a dungeon with a few single beds. A cabinet sits at the far side of the room. Through its glass doors, one can see vials of all sizes. There is an operating table against a wall. Sheets beneath it are caked black with blood.

I try to rise onto my elbows, but I'm still too weak. Finally, I whisper, "Is this a hospital? Are you a nurse?"

To silence me, she puts a finger to her lips. Her furtive glances down the hall assure her that no one is within listening distance. Her excuse to lean in is to place a pillow behind my head. In stilted English, she murmurs, "I am *la religiosa.*" Noting my blank look, she thinks for a moment, then adds, "A nun. El Maestro allows us to administer to those prisoners he sees fit."

The memory of the executions comes back to me. "Why me?"

She shrugs. "It is said that he saves you for something special. I do not know why."

"He is a drug lord, is he not?"

Even as she nods, she drops her head in shame. "*Sí.* But sometimes, to do the work of God, one must commune with the Devil."

"What is your name?"

"*Sor* Juana Inés."

"Please, Sister—*Sor*, allow me to give you a note so that you may mail it for me."

Her face turns white at the thought.

"Or if you have access to the Internet—"

"No, I cannot!" The fear in her dark eyes pierces my soul.

But it is she who shivers as she walks to the cabinet. She pulls out a prescription pad and a pencil.

I write down a fake name assigned to a post office box in Los Angeles. It is always monitored by an Acme operative.

The message to be sent is a mere sentence, coded. It simply reads:

Vacationing in Canada. Intoxicating! Staying with the bandleader. Will be home 01/30 --Rapaiso

Donna, like me, you know the codebook backward and forward. A detention situation is no vacation. The opposite of Canada is Mexico. The clue as to who is holding me captive is the term bandleader. An additional clue is the exclamation following "intoxicating" which should tip off our cryptographers that illegal substances are his business. The date is my birthday, so that Acme has a clue as to who sent this communiqué; and finally, *Rapaiso* is an anagram for my location.

She folds the note and sticks in under her wimple.

She spends the next twenty minutes tidying up. When she leaves, she nods goodbye.

A HALF-HOUR LATER, I AM JOSTLED FROM MY COT BY TWO guards. They drag me out to the prisoners' courtyard. It is filled with men who, like me, are dressed simply in stained gray prison garb.

And like me, the men are captivated by what they see in the middle of the yard: Sister Juana Inés, kneeling in prayer, her rosary in her hand. Her eyes are closed. Her lips move in prayer.

Oscar holds a gun to her head. When he looks up at the rooftop, I follow his gaze.

Two other nuns and a priest are on the roof with El Maestro, pleading with him to let her go, telling him that the young novice made an innocent mistake, and it will never happen again.

He silences them with the threat to have them join her, and laughs riotously when the women collapse at his feet in prayer. The priest looks down at Sister Juana Inés and makes the sign of the cross.

Now that it is daylight, I can have a good look at the *narco* known as El Maestro. He is tall. His bespoke suit of white linen can't hide his hefty build. His eyes are deep-set, thanks to the ridge of bone and flesh that seems to protrude from his forehead, truly a cruel trick of genetics. His teeth are much too white within his too wide mouth.

He grins down at me, and in perfect English, declares loud enough for all to hear, "Hey, *Gringo*! Did you not think that El Maestro has eyes and ears everywhere? The death of *la religiosa* is now a permanent stain upon your soul."

In unison, the prisoners turn to glare at me.

What a fool I was! But, of course, the whole place is under video surveillance.

He throws my note to the wind. It flutters to the ground.

El Maestro snaps his fingers.

Oscar puts the muzzle of his gun to her forehead.

Sor Juana Inés's blood draws a psychedelic pattern in the dry earth. A piece of her skull lands at my feet.

Oscar laughs at the look of horror on my face.

My response is to charge him.

Before he can lift his gun for another shot, I knock him to the ground, landing hard on his chest.

His head hits the hard earth with a thud. His gun goes flying from his hand.

When my thumb stabs his eye, his howl echoes off the prison yard walls.

The man on the roof shouts, *"Ponlo en el infierno!"*

What...*hellhole?*

It takes five guards to pull me off of Oscar. I am carried

by the guards toward an iron grate in the ground. One of the men pulls it to one side, while two others throw down a rope ladder. A prisoner lumbers up, gasping for air.

The guards toss me into the hole, pulling up the ladder behind them.

I land in the last guy's pile of shit.

Oscar whimpers as he gets onto his feet. Having channeled his pain into anger, he tosses *Sor* Juana Inés's rosary in after me.

7

"He" Time

Believe it or not, Wife, your concern over his periodic disappearances shouldn't be cause for alarm. Sometimes, he just needs a little "he" time. Just the facts, ma'am:

- *Fact #1: A little mystery between husbands and wives is important, if only because it keeps the sexual tension alive.*

(However, if it turns out that the reason he's gone has something to do with his urge to satisfy his sexual tensions with others, feel free to introduce him to a different kind of tension—say, fear. Tip: Try holding a semi-automatic between his legs.)

- *Fact #2: Counter his mysterious disappearances with a few of your own! That's not to say you should*

book a week-long trip to the Grand Wailea
in Maui…

Oh, heck, sure you should! He'll find out where you are soon
enough: when he gets the bill.

- *Fact #3: Remember, he had a life before he met you:*
  with a job, friends, and family. You should trust that
  the time he spends away from you continues to
  cement these relationships.

However, if it turns out that he has a secret life, no doubt
you'll make sure that "cement" plays a role in his life in a
whole different way. (Tip: after planting him, cover him with
an "energetically modified" cement brand. These are strong,
economically priced, and have the added advantage of being
better for the environment!)

WE HAVEN'T SEEN ERIC SINCE VARICK, GUNTER, OR I CAME
onto his private plane at Oakland Airport. From the time
we reached cruising altitude, he's been in the plane's
private bedroom with the door closed.

Yes, I'm biting my nails to know who has him on the
phone, and what is being said.

I hear the murmur of his voice, but I can't make out
Eric's words because Gunter has the television tuned to a
porn flick. When Eric finally emerges, he greets me with a

big smile on his face. "Konstantin was a bit disappointed that you left the party so early."

Varick pours a celebratory drink for his lord and master: a forty-year-old single-malt scotch. But instead of joining his favorite lap dog for a toast, he takes the chair beside mine.

Hugo notices this too, and snickers at his colleague's expense.

Eric's admonishment gets nothing more than a shrug from me. "I delivered the goods. He's lucky I didn't tear his arm out of its socket when he copped a feel."

"Such a quaint American term." His eyes zero in on my breasts. "Beauty is a terrible cross to bear."

"A missing husband is a bigger one. Tell me, Mr. Weber, what is the second of my four assignments?"

"We are on our way there now." His gaze shifts to the plane's closest window. We've been flying in a southeasterly direction. "We're headed to your old stomping grounds—Guantánamo Bay. A dear friend of mine is getting released today from prison," Eric continues. "You are to escort him out."

I wince at the name of the United States' notorious military prison, which is the home of captured terrorists. The last time I was there I was roofied by Carl, and left to take the fall for his escape—naked, in the broiling sun on a nearby tropical island.

I'm surprised that I don't still have the tan marks to prove it.

Noting my frown, he adds, "Not to worry! Nine years

in captivity has taken its toll on him. He is a broken man —in other words, nothing at all like the few days to be experienced by your husband."

"Oh? I have no proof of that. For all I know, you've already killed him."

"Trust, my pet! We must have trust if our little arrangement is going to work."

"I need some show of good faith. Let me speak to him at least."

His face goes blank, as if the stakes in this poker game just doubled.

Truth is, he holds the high cards. We both know it.

The silence between us grows with each nautical mile. Finally, he says, "Should you succeed on this next assignment, you'll have your proof."

I'm sure he sees the relief in my eyes.

Does he catch the shadow of concern there as well, when a moment later, I realize that I can't give him what he wants?

So that he can't, I force my lips into a smile. "Thank you, Eric. Doing so would certainly earn my trust. And I'm sure that the last mission proves I'm worthy of yours. What is your friend's name?"

"Ramadan Abdullah Shallah. Surely you've heard of him."

"Yes, of course. He was the leader of the al-Qaeda cells in Syria. Supposedly, he was also the treasurer for the whole organization. I guess he knows where a few very important bodies are buried, not to mention a few offshore bank accounts."

"Very good!" He claps, as if I've done some sort of parlor trick. "Although, I must say, that last summation is an urban legend." In mock shock, he clicks his tongue. "It's not nice to repeat rumors, Mrs. Craig."

I shrug. "If anyone knows for sure, I guess it's you." Of course, I don't believe him. The Quorum has long been Al-Qaeda's chief funding source.

Ryan seconds my supposition when he mutters into my earbud, "Political pressure to release Shallah is coming from the United Arab Emirates. POTUS thinks they want to torture him so that he'll lead them to the money. We've given it our best, so why not let them have a go at him? He's been embedded with GPS and audio chips, so whatever they hear, we will too."

"Sounds like a plan," I say out loud. "One thing, Eric. Why do I need to be his escort?"

Eric laughs, as if I've said something clever. "Why, my dear, I certainly can't be seen with him, now can I?" He motions toward the bedroom. "There was nothing appropriate amongst your belongings for such a momentous occasion. While you were enjoying yourself at the Russian Consulate, I took it upon myself to pick up a little something for you. A whole closet full of little somethings, in fact. But for this assignment, I've laid out my own favorite on the bed in the smaller sleeping suite—which is at your disposal as well. We land in Cuba in another five hours."

"Call out if you need someone to zip you up," Varick taunts me as I walk to the bedroom.

It's on the tip of my tongue to ask him if he'd like to try it on instead, but knowing Eric, it's expensive. If so, I may want to hold onto it.

Then again, maybe not. I'm sure that the memories associated with it are ones I'd prefer to forget.

I DON'T KNOW WHY ERIC HAS GONE HOG WILD WITH MY clothing budget. I guess he sees me as his own little Barbie Doll. Go figure.

The navy linen suit he purchased for me fits me like a glove. Its midi skirt is pencil thin, with a slit in the back. The matching jacket has white cap sleeves and a white Peter Pan collar. Its large white buttons run up the back.

He's even purchased white pumps and a matching handbag.

Inside the bag are business cards that identify me as an associate of a major international law firm that specializes in defense litigation, as well as sunglasses, non-prescription glasses, and a passport with the name Helen Miriam Isaacs. A few years have been shaved off my age.

If Eric is trying to earn brownie points, he'll have to do better than that.

No need to pack my newly acquired Glock, since I won't be allowed to carry it into Gitmo. That's okay, it's not as if I'm going there to kill someone.

Then again, the night is young.

THE GUANTÁNAMO GUEST RECEPTION AREA IS JUST AS I remember it: clean, but depressingly gray.

In other words, foreboding.

My passport is scrutinized. I might have popped up under my real name if the facility had a facial recognition program. The last time I was here was to testify against my ex-husband Carl Stone, whose own acts of counterespionage and terrorism may have put him in some sort of Gitmo Hall of Fame.

Ramadan Abdullah Shallah's name would certainly be near the top of the list as well.

Shallah's release papers are three inches thick. As instructed, I scan them quickly, then print Helen's initials on every page, or her signature where indicated.

When that ordeal is over, I wait a half-hour. Every moment there makes my skin crawl.

Finally, Shallah is brought out. He wears traditional Middle-Eastern garb. It is worn, but clean. Most men come out of Gitmo looking one of two ways: broken, or resolved to live up to their international reputations. From the cold stare I get, I'm willing to guess the latter.

I hand him one of my business cards.

"They send a woman—a Jewess no less?" He looks heavenward.

"This way, Mr. Shallah," I point to the door.

He says nothing, but starts out in front of me. He doesn't open the door for me.

That's okay. Gitmo isn't a finishing school. And Shallah's orders for the jihadist raids on so many innocent children, women, and men proves that he's no gentleman.

It's a five-minute drive from the prison to the tarmac. Our driver, Hugo, seems to be in no rush—a shame, considering that I must spend it sitting next to one of the world's most despised men.

When we pull onto the tarmac, there is another private jet next to ours.

Eric waits outside the jet. Varick and Gunter stand beside him. It's hot enough that his jacket is off. He wears a gun in a shoulder holster.

When the car stops, Gunter opens Shallah's door. He walks over and shakes Eric's hand. They are old friends indeed.

At that moment, the door to the other plane opens. Two bearded men in white robes and traditional Arab headdress walk down the jet's air stairs.

When he sees them, Shallah's face turns red with fury. Angrily, he turns to Eric. "You German monster! You sold me out!"

Ryan commands Arnie, "Can you pull up facial recognition traits on those men?"

"On it," Arnie answers. In a few seconds he shouts,

"Holy shit! The one in front is Abu Ali al-Anbari, the second in command of ISIL in Syria!"

"Eric just handed him over to his enemies," Ryan murmurs. "This is even better for us! Shallah is going to take us directly to their covert headquarters!"

Not if Shallah can help it. He lunges toward Eric. It turns out that what he's really after is Varick's gun. Grabbing it, he swings it around to Al-Anbari.

"Donna, if he kills Al-Anbari, he's the next to die, and we have nothing!"

"Got it," I whisper.

Gunter is too slow to react when I strip the gun from his back holster. My shot slams into Shallah's hand, shattering bone.

He drops Varick's gun with a howl.

Al-Anbari's bodyguards hustle him onto the plane.

"Bravo, my little soldier girl!" Eric's look of admiration makes me want to puke. I could have taken out one of ISIL's two most notorious leaders. Instead, I let him walk.

As if reading my mind, Ryan whispers in my ear, "It's all good, Donna. Remember, we're playing a long game."

I know better. I'm not playing at all. The stakes are much too high:

Jack's life.

8

Jack's Diary, Day 4

Dear Donna,

It's been two days since I was tossed into El Maestro's hellhole—an apt name, considering how hot it is in this part of Mexico. One would think that, twenty feet beneath the earth's dry crust, it would be at least a few degrees cooler, but no. I am inflamed by gusts of scorched air, as if I'm stuck in an inferno.

Perhaps El Maestro is right, that this is a fitting penance for the death of a nun.

Sound also travels to my underground chamber. Both the prisoners and their guards forget I am down here below the grate, as invisible as a ghost. Their gossip floats down to me on acrid waves of heat, muttered in hushed tones.

From the guards, I learn that El Maestro is now one of

the top drug lords in the country, and is honing in on territory currently held by the Sinaloa Cartel, which is Mexico's biggest drug organization and the world's biggest meth supplier. Apparently, he has recently found the funding to buy enough political clout to make a dent in their monopoly.

My guess is that the Quorum is his new bank. Otherwise, why would I be here, and why would he have stopped Oscar from executing me?

Some of my fellow prisoners are born and raised here and used to work in El Maestro's poppy fields. The pods of this colorful flowering plant are harvested for its sap, which hardens into *goma*—gum-like balls. Their crime was to get caught smuggling out *goma* in the hope that its sales would allow them to leave the region and make a new life for themselves and their families, whose world never went beyond the tiny villages located in these remote valleys tucked deep in the Sierra Madre Occidental Mountain Range, on the western coast of the Gulf of California.

Others are *narco* foot soldiers who found themselves on the wrong side of El Maestro's territorial battles with the other cartels. He tortures them for intel on his enemies. If the price is right, he trades them to their leaders. But even those who leave do so with his mark on them: he carves his initials into their feet with a knife.

The lives of these men are living hells. But likely, not for long. They know that, eventually, they'll pay for their crimes with them.

Today, one of them—once a highly ranked lieutenant in the Juárez Cartel—was accused by another prisoner of being a snitch. He admitted he was taken to El Maestro's palace, on the other side of the plaza. There, he was given an ultimatum: sell out his chief, or lose an eye.

He chose the eye, he declared. "But I still have the nose."

"What does that mean?" his accuser asked.

"It means that I know a meth lab when I smell it. Like *vinagre, sí?*"

"*Ah, sí.*"

"Well, guess what? He has one in the bowels of his palace."

"*¡No mames!*" His newfound admirer was dumbfounded at that thought. Most of the *narcos* grow, produce, and distribute far away from their private palaces. In other words, you don't shit where you eat.

"*¡Es un pendejo!* To his mind, he doesn't make product. He is making art! He calls it *'Paraíso Azul'.*" One-Eyed Juan snorted at the thought. "And all artists need a studio. His laboratory is right there. It is why we…"

Suddenly they stopped talking. A minute went by before Juan kicked the grate high above my head. In English, he asked, "Are you still alive, *Gringo*?"

I didn't answer.

A stream of piss arched its way down between the rails of the grate, catching me in the eye. After One-Eyed Juan emptied his bladder, he shouted down to me: "Your life will be worth nothing when you get out. Better you should die in the hole."

He's right. Every day, someone vows to kill me. An angel was murdered because of me. I didn't pull the trigger, but I might as well have.

9

Teamwork

Wives, a relationship takes both of you to make it work. Or as the saying goes, there is no "I" in "teamwork."

Let me spell out a few other things for you:

There is no "you" in boys' night out, so get over it. Or else give him a better reason to stay home.

There is no "be" in "reality"—as in, "It may not be all you hoped, so make do with what you've got." If you feel you can train him to be different, sure, give it a try. (Helpful Hint: This is where a whip and a cattle prod come in handy.)

And finally, there is no "see" in "flaws." We all have them. If his get on your nerves, cut him some slack. You may not think so now, but as time goes by, they'll grow on you.

Either that, or your aim will improve. There is a "u" in gun!

$\sim$

I'M QUIET THE WHOLE WAY BACK TO LOS ANGELES. HAD Ryan not been covertly involved, I'd now be at the top of the FBI's Most Wanted List.

Eric is too smart to bother me. However, he takes out his frustration on Varick. Slapping him hard, he growls, "You fool! Exposing your firearm to the man! What if he had shot the client? Worse yet, what if he'd shot *me?*"

"Oh, give it a break, Eric! Of course his jacket was off. It was hotter than Hades on that tarmac. Besides, all's well that ends well." I know I shouldn't get involved, but I've just saved his life and his biggest account, so he owes me.

Time to collect. "I've successfully completed the second assignment. Put me on the phone with my husband, like you promised."

Instead, he slaps my face. "How dare you talk to me like that in front of my underlings!"

My head reels back from the blow. It split my lip. A few drops of blood fall onto my suit jacket.

Fuck, it's ruined.

For that matter, so is any hope I have that Eric will keep his word to me.

This new reality must be reflected in my face because Eric's fury dissipates almost as quickly as it appeared. In its place is a benign calmness. "Demerits, my dear. Yours have earned you one more assignment before I allow you to talk to your beloved."

He heads toward his private suite, closing the door behind him.

"Think of Jack." Emma's whisper puts everything in perspective again.

"Hand me your jacket so that I can dab it with an ice cube. The blood will come right off." Varick holds out his hand for it.

His concern is touching. Still, I know better than to presume I have an ally in him.

I turn around so that he can unbutton the jacket for me. When I turn back around, I notice that he's not admiring me, but the cut of the jacket.

Figures.

On the other hand, Gunter's eyes narrow in on my knockers like heat-seeking missiles.

It's as close as he's going to get to them. From the way he's drooling, I guess he knows this too.

ONLY AFTER WE'VE RECEIVED NOTICE FROM THE COCKPIT THAT we've gotten clearance to land at Van Nuys Airport does Eric come out of his lair. "Lady and gents, we have a traitor in our midst. I've just learned that one of our operatives is a double agent—"

I may be able to keep a poker face, but I feel my heart sink into my gut. The Glock I stole off Konstanin is hidden behind my bed, so at this moment, it does me no good. If Eric calls out the dogs, I'll have to steal Varick's, again.

But this time I won't be hanging around to see him get bitch-slapped.

"—and he happens to be here tonight."

Eric said *he.*

Works for me. It can't be me he suspects.

"Mrs. Craig, you have your third trial."

"And what would that be, exactly?"

"His extermination." Eric changes the television's channel from Gunter's never-ending soccer game to *Entertainment Tonight.* The host, Nancy O'Dell, is interviewing Daniel Parker, the star of a movie: "The Lorne Conundrum," the latest release in a very successful film franchise about a superspy who has been burned, and must travel the world to escape the wrath of old colleagues and enemies.

Talk about art imitating life.

"Damn it," Ryan mutters in my ear. "Daniel is one of ours!"

Yikes.

"It looks as if he's touring with the release of the movie," I point out to Eric. "When will I have the opportunity?"

"Tonight, in fact—prior to the premiere which is happening tonight, at the Kodak Theater." He tosses me a small vial filled with a clear liquid. "It's Propranolol—a beta-blocker. Too much—that is, the amount in here ingested—and he'll be standing at the Pearly Gates."

"How will I pass it to him?"

"My pet, like most of us, he's a creature of habit. He and his wife, Isabella, like to stay at the Chateau Marmont when they come to Los Angeles. Part of his red carpet ritual is to order a celebratory martini at the Marmont's bar. You'll be there to put it in his drink. He'll drop dead before they roll the opening credits. Should make for quite a Tinseltown legend." He nods toward the bedroom. "The regular barkeep has met with an unfortunate incident. We've arranged for you to take his place. You'll find your uniform in your bedroom closet. By the way, Varick will be sitting at the bar, so should you get cold feet—or for that matter, try to run—you won't get very far."

Varick bares his much-too-white teeth at me.

"Duly noted," I assure them.

I hope Varick orders a drink. I've got just the perfect chaser for it.

"Team, any thoughts?" I ask, standing in front of the closet door's mirror. The white shirt that is part of my uniform fits tight across my chest. I'm to wear it with black pants, a bowtie, and suspenders.

"I like you better in brighter colors," Abu weighs in.

"Not about my ensemble, smart ass. I mean about how I keep our man alive."

"We substitute your vial for another," Ryan declares. "Emma will also be behind the bar. Donna, put the vial in the right hand side of the ice chest. Emma will leave the fake Propranolol on the left side. She'll toss it down the bar's sink. That way, there can be no mix-up."

"Will do, boss." I can tell by Emma's hurt tone that

she's still smarting over the mix-up with the thumb drives.

"I'm sure Daniel Parker can pull off a fake heart attack, but what happens when the medics are called to revive him?"

"I call dibs on being the onsite doctor!" Arnie begs. "Ryan, what do you say? I have to revive him anyway, right? And besides, I know every episode of *Grey's Anatomy* by heart—"

"Sold—but only because beggars can't be choosers," Ryan mutters grudgingly.

"One last question." I sigh. "Won't dying in public put an end to his acting career?"

Everyone is silent.

I wait a full minute. Then: "Um…hello?"

"Fake death beats the alternative," Ryan mutters.

He's got a point.

I'm glad I won't be there when Ryan breaks the news to one of the world's most celebrated actors that his career is over.

Daniel's eyes are just as blue in person as they are on any sixty-foot-tall movie screen. When he asks for a dirty martini, I just have to ask: "Shaken not stirred, am I right?"

He chuckles as he rolls his eyes. "Yeah, sure, it's not as

if I've never heard *that* one before. Sorry, that's the other guy."

I reach for a martini glass. "You're all dressed up. What's the occasion?"

"Tonight is my movie's premiere. I'm celebrating." His smile is grim. The sadness in his eyes is proof that he's been told the news that he's been burned. He puts a finger to his lips. "*Shhh.* Don't tell my wife when she gets here, but I'd like a double."

"No problem. In fact, since you're celebrating, I'm sure management won't mind me breaking open our most expensive vodka: Imperial Collection Super Premium." I wink, as if I'm keeping his secret.

From the code word—the vodka brand—he knows who I am.

Varick, however, is clueless—nothing new there. He sits a few stools down, nursing an appletini that Emma made for him. She wanted to slip him a roofie, but calmer heads prevailed: Ryan's.

As planned, the second vial is in the top left corner of the ice chest. Before picking it up, I shove the real stuff deep under the shavings on the right.

He turns so that Daniel can't watch me make his drink, but Varick can. He watches as I pour the contents of Emma's vial into a martini shaker. Next, I add the vermouth, the vodka, and a splash of olive brine.

I nod at Varick before turning around with the shaker in order to pour the concoction into Daniel's glass.

At the same time, Emma pours the Propranolol down the sink.

Daniel holds up his glass to me. "Here's to knocking them dead," he declares, then takes a sip.

"Amen," Varick mutters.

By the time Daniel's wife, Isabella, joins him, he's on his second drink. The raven-haired beauty's gown is Givenchy. Her jewels are Tiffany. Her smile is genuine. I presume that's because he hasn't yet broken the news to her that his acting career is dead.

Well, better it than him.

By the time Daniel's publicists comes to whisk them away to the theater, the film's premiere is already under way. The red carpet stops where the sidewalk meets Hollywood Boulevard, but the line of fans for Daniel Parker and the *Lorne* movies goes several blocks in either direction.

Varick waits fifteen minutes before giving me the high sign that it's time to move on. I excuse myself to Emma, claiming the need for a bathroom break. She waves me on. She's pouring tall goblets of red wine for a couple of reality stars. They pose in the hope that someone will recognize them. When Varick walks toward the door, one of them waves him down. "Don't I know you?" she asks coyly.

As he preens, it's on the tip of my tongue to say, be

careful what you wish for.

Hugo has the limo waiting outside for us. Eric is in back, dressed in a tux. With his imperious bearing, he could pass for a movie producer or a studio head. Noting my bartender garb, the hotel's valet gives me a strange look. I guess he thinks I'm getting my big break. For all the acting I've done since Jack's kidnapping, I should be up for an Academy Award.

ERIC HAS THE TOWN CAR'S TELEVISION TUNED TO THE LIVE telecast of the premiere. Daniel's swan song happens just as he's made it to the end of the red carpet. From when he first stepped from the limousine until he reached the first step on the theater's tall staircase, he was the consummate star. His grin is joyous. He took his time with the paparazzi, allowing them to take lots of shots of him with his arm around Isabella. The few times his arm left her waist, it was to clasp his hands in front, humbly. He ambled over the red velvet rope in order to talk to fans, sign autographs, and pose with them for selfies.

"If I didn't know better, I'd say he knew this was his last time to walk the red carpet," Eric murmured.

I did know better, but he wasn't hearing it from me.

The heart attack happens when he is halfway up the theater's grand staircase. It isn't too theatrical: a stumble, a clutch of the chest, then down on one side.

Isabelle stares. Suddenly, she screams. Kneeling beside

him, she flips him onto his back so that she can loosen his tie.

In no time, Arnie is beside them. He wears a white medic's coat and quickly pulls a stethoscope from his pocket. He goes through the paces of checking for a pulse and trying to resuscitate the star.

Arnie is soon joined by Abu and Dominic, who are dressed as EMTs. They put Daniel on a stretcher, and carry him out a side entrance, leaving the crowd hysterical and the reporters babbling excitedly with their eyewitness accounts.

By the time we get back to our hotel, the L'Ermitage, Daniel's death has been formally announced.

"The box office receipts should go through the roof," Eric proclaims. "I'm so glad I invested in the movie."

I can't believe my ears. "Is that the real reason you killed him?"

Eric chuckles. "No, of course not! But, this is a wonderful example that things are better off not left to fate."

I can't wait for the chance to prove to him that he's not really God.

GUNTER IS GUARDING THE DOOR TO MY ROOM. WE ARE ON the top floor of the hotel, so Eric is pretty sure I won't jump out the window.

Why should I? I'd much rather take a nice warm bath.

As the water runs, through my earbuds I listen to Ryan explaining to Daniel and Isabella that he's sorry about the demise of Daniel's career.

"Me too," Daniel grunts. "It was what I lived for. With plastic surgery, I can go back undercover—"

"No, no, no!" Isabella shouts. "No more spycraft! Don't you see? We're being given a second chance!"

"What am I supposed to do, exactly?" he counters. "A spook is what I am, damn it!"

"You're an actor, first and foremost," she insists.

"You're wrong! I grew to hate it!"

"No! What you hated was being a *star*." Her voice is calm and true. "Just think, Danny: no more exhausting premieres and silly interviews. You'll no longer be tied to one iconic role with endless, unrealistic plots! Best of all, you can do theater again, and small independent films." Her sobs choke her words. "Darling, finally, we can live like normal people who love our art for art's sake, no matter how successful or challenging it may be!"

"But, Isabella, dearest, as an actor, I've got an even shorter shelf life. I'm too old to start over—"

"Isabella is right," Ryan interrupts. "You can start over again, in, say, Australia. It's a wonderful pipeline for actors. And besides, plastic surgery will shave a few years off your age."

The silence goes on for so long that at first I think I've lost the feed.

Finally, Daniel sighs. "Alright." He chuckles. "And all

this time I thought you abhorred my leaping into bed with all those beautiful women!"

"Oh…that?" She laughs. "It's a charade! You love playing to the cameras. But you love me even more."

"And I always will." The fervency in his voice is proof that he's willing to give up the game of spy versus spy for her.

Can he just lead a normal life? For some spooks, it's a fantasy. For others, it's a nightmare.

I tried to get out. I couldn't.

With all that has happened over the past few days, I wonder if Jack would do the same.

I guess I'll know when I see him.

His decision will be mine as well.

10

Jack's Diary, Day 5

DEAR DONNA,

This morning the guards finally let me out of my hellhole.

From the passage of light sifting through the grates far above my head, my guess was that it was my home for the past two days. You'd think that since I'd been subsisting on only rice and beans that I'd be weak, but no. I guess nothing energizes you more than knowing that your every move can make the difference between life and death.

My tormentor, the one called Oscar, delivered my reprieve. "Gringo! Climb out if you can!" His next remarks, in Spanish, were muttered to the other guards in a voice too low for me to catch his every word. The ones I do catch let me know exactly where I stand with him. He calls me *cabrón* (motherfucker) and *chingadera* (piece of shit).

It wasn't going to be easy keeping my cool. But I had to, Donna, if I wanted to stay alive.

When I reached the top rung, at Oscar's command, the guards lifted me under my armpits and tossed me onto the ground, on my knees. They laughed raucously as I coughed on the clouds of dust swirling around me. It took a few moments for my eyes to adjust to the bright sunlight.

The next thing I knew, other prisoners were circling me like vultures.

I stood up. I shifted my gaze from one to the other, all the while flexing my hands: the universal gesture for, *just try to take a piece of me, asshole.*

They taunted and growled, but no one stepped forward.

Oscar pulled something from his pocket: a gold coin. He held it up for all to see.

The prisoners froze, as if mesmerized by it.

Oscar flipped it into the air.

It landed at the feet of the largest prisoner—a muscular brute who hovered at six-and a half feet, his fists the size of hams. He picked it up. His eyes grew large when he realized what he held in his large palm. *"¡Diez dólares en dinero Americano!"*

He bit the ten-dollar coin, as if that could prove it was legitimate. Satisfied, his eyes shifted to Oscar. *"¿Para mi?"*

"Sí—por el precio de un ojo."

I heard the shortest guard, Jaime, exclaim in Spanish, "Oscar, what have you done? El Maestro said punish the gringo, but do not kill him!"

So, El Maestro wanted to keep me alive? I didn't know why, but at this point I didn't care, since it was certainly what I wanted to hear.

Oscar didn't necessarily see it that way. "Fair punishment is an eye for an eye, no?" He lifted his eye patch to show Jaime my handiwork: a hollow eye socket. I watch as his one good eye seeks me out. "I can't help it if he gets killed by one of the other prisoners."

He tossed a jackknife at Big Boy's feet. It stuck in the dirt.

The other prisoners eased just far enough away to form a circle around us.

Big Boy picked it up and flicked it open. When he turned to face me, it was as if he'd already won the lottery.

At this point, I wasn't scared. I was ready. I wasn't going to let this asshole stand in the way of getting home to you, Donna.

No one would. I swore to that.

BIG BOY'S ARMS WERE SO LONG THAT I BARELY GOT OUT OF the way of his first slash. The knife missed my gut by a hair's breadth.

I blocked his second strike—a lateral one—with my forearm.

I kept blocking his wild slashes while my eyes adjusted to daylight for the first time in two days.

As we fought, some of the men cheered. Others wagered their precious cigarettes on which of us would be the last man standing. Those who had experienced his prison yard bullying or weren't impressed with his lumbering gait put their bets—in this case, cigarettes—on me.

I had no intention of letting them down.

Angered, Big Boy's next joust nicked my chest, but I tripped him as he lunged forward. Before he could recover his stride, I grabbed his wrist from behind and twisted his arm—fast, hard, and straight up behind his back. He howled as his arm broke.

Instinctively, he opened his palm.

I snatched the knife from his hand.

Before he knew it, I slashed his throat from ear to ear.

Gargling blood, he fell backward.

He was dead before he hit the ground.

The mob's reaction was silence.

Above us, on the balcony of the palace, someone was clapping.

It was El Maestro himself. I don't know how long he was standing there, but it couldn't have been too long because when I turned around, his smile faded.

Seeing this, all the blood left Oscar's face.

El Maestro motioned to the guard beside him. The

man leaned closer in order to hear his boss's order, then turned and left the balcony. A moment later, he was striding toward us. In Spanish, he asked, "The gringo: who allowed him to fight?"

The prison guards shifted their gazes to Oscar.

By now, Oscar was trembling. Finally, he raised his head—and his eye patch.

From the balcony, El Maestro chortled mirthlessly at the guard's belligerence. But just as quickly, his grin curdled into a snarl. "If you were looking for retribution, perhaps you should have exacted the punishment your-self. Instead, you put another one of my assets at risk. Your presumption didn't pay off. For your stupidity, you must now pay the price." He raised both hands into the air. "*Combate a muerte.*"

A death match.

The term flowed from the lips of the prisoners, as if they were attached by the same stream of consciousness. In no time, they were chanting it together: *combate a muerte, combate a muerte, combate a muerte…*

El Maestro's bodyguard wrenched Oscar's rifle from his arm, then shoved him in my direction. Oscar and I stared at each other. Another fight to the death?

We had no choice.

He realized this the same time as me.

I could see it in his eyes: the instinct to run away.

Mine was to kill the son of a bitch who put me in that hole, and tried to have me killed.

To stop him from acting on his instinct, I reached

down and scooped up a handful of dust, which I then tossed in his one good eye. Blinded, he didn't see my kick to his gut coming. It put him on his ass.

I landed on his chest, hard with both knees. That alone knocked the wind out of him. With my hands throttling his neck, he never got it back.

The one eye left in his head finally opened, bulging as his life left his body.

Minutes after his death, it still gave me pleasure to wring his neck.

When I finally stopped, I closed my eyes and lifted my head high in order to see you, my dear Donna, in my mind's eye. Your smile reflected the hot white joy that comes with a successful mission, but that is immediately eclipsed by the darkness of our acts, all casting heavy shadows on our souls.

Are the lives we take worth the price?

When I open my eyes, I find that I'm staring up at my host, El Maestro.

He nodded to the bodyguard at my side.

The next thing I knew, the other prisoners were being herded back into their pens. On the other hand, Jaime and another man goose-stepped me in the bodyguard's wake into the palace.

I was put in a proper room, with a bed, a dresser, and a real bathroom. One of the guards flushed the toilet and nodded, impressed. In English, Jaime murmured, "It goes down all the way, not like the crapper in the guards' quarters."

Because I'd never heard him mutter a word before, I couldn't help but stare at him now. "Your English is pretty good."

He shrugged. "It should be. I grew up in Fresno."

"Then what the hell are you doing here?"

"Surviving until I can get home. I brought my mother home, here to Paraíso, for her sister's funeral. Someone stole our passports and my driver's license."

"The American Embassy should be able to help you."

"Not if your passport was fake to begin with." He shrugged. "My cousin, Alfredo, is El Maestro's chief of security. He got me a job here. Beats being a heroin mule."

He had a point.

I looked around the room. There were bars on the window. I'd noticed a bolt on the exterior of the door. Still, for some reason, El Maestro felt I should be rewarded.

Taking two lives won me this privilege.

I have a feeling that a higher price is yet to be paid.

I will kill whoever stands in my way for the chance to stay alive and come back to you.

11

The Couple Who Plays Together Stays Together

The best way to keep him at your side is to learn to love the things he does! For example:

- *Tip #1: Watching Sports. He's got his favorite spot on your couch, and your poor sofa has the sunken cushion to prove it. If the most prevalent sound in your home is that of a cheering crowd or a sports announcer who just won't shut up, don't let it drive you crazy. Instead, learn the names of his favorite teams, their players, and the players' pertinent stats. Doing so allows you to learn the lingo of sports. You now have the perfect entrée into his world!*

However, if it turns out to be just as boring as you thought, don't point your gun at your head—or even his! Shoot the one thing standing between you and your man: the TV. By the time his new jumbo-screen HDTV gets there, the two of you will have had the opportunity to have a real conversation—even if it started with your apology for being such a great shot.

- *Tip #2: Playing Sports. With the TV splattered to smithereens, he now has no reason to sit on that couch. There is no better time than now to take him into the great outdoors!*

You'd think his love of sports would translate into some excellent athletic skills, wouldn't you? Wives, please don't be disappointed if his throwing arm turns out to be as weak as an aging widow's. Put things in perspective: the only thing he uses it for is to reach for the remote.

Instead of pointing this out, do what you'd do with a child: encourage him to try, try again. And when he does, do your best not to snicker at the results. (Remember: your turn is next...)

- *Tip #3: Being a Good Sport. Couples coziness can best be accomplished with some contact sports. No one says you have to go outside the bedroom to watch him run all the bases, or to make that incredible touchdown and win your heart. And if he needs a little coaching, well hey, that's your best role —as you've already proven in all other areas of his life.*

"MY DEAR MRS. CRAIG, IT SEEMS THAT AN ASSIGNMENT HAS fallen into our laps that is ideal for your mélange of talents." Eric takes his place beside me on the settee facing the fireplace in his private study inside of a five-bedroom residence suite at the Montage Hotel in Beverly Hills.

Just hearing the term "mélange of talents" gives me a headache. I'd like to use one of them now: say, wringing his neck with my bare hands. Instead, I rub my temples. "Oh? Do tell."

"We have quite a lucrative retainer in the retrieval of China's fugitives who find themselves stateside." He looks skyward, as if perhaps he might find these missing persons somewhere in the firmament above us. "One is currently a scientist working in Lockheed Martin on its RQ-170 unmanned aerial vehicles."

"Ah yes, drones."

"Precisely. Well, it seems that he's decided that Arizona's sunny skies are an improvement over Beijing's smoggy haze."

"Go figure."

"My sentiments exactly." Eric coughs, as if making his point. "You are tasked with convincing the target, Wang Chen, to remember his duty to his native country."

"By that, I presume you mean bring home the bacon—ergo, the diagrams for the RQ-170, so that they might have a start on reverse-engineering its radar system, in the hope of taking down one or two of our aircraft, like the F-35?"

"My, my, you *are* a smart lass!" Eric pinches my cheek. "Sadly, the Chinese are several decades behind your industrious country in developing a similar radar system. China's premier, Li Keqiang, has this fantasy that it will happen during his administration. All the more reason that he desperately covets any and all things committed to Chen's photographic memory."

The last thing we need is for the drone's radar system to end up in the hands of the Chinese.

Obviously, Ryan is of like mind. "Dominic will be shadowing you. By the time you intercept Chen, we'll have his long-distance travel plans covered."

"Super," I say out loud. "Well then, we'd better hurry. Coups are *de rigueur* in that neck o' the woods, are they not?" I stretch in order to move out of pinching range. "So, why me as opposed to, say Gunter, or Varick, for that matter?"

He lets his eyes drop below my neck. "You see, Wang enjoys strip clubs—one in particular: The Coyote Cabaret, in Goodyear, Arizona." His brows do a happy dance. "And all too conveniently, several of the strippers have come down with colds, so they're hiring."

"Better than herpes, I imagine."

"Perhaps you're right. In any event, they have an opening, and you're elected."

"I got more votes than Gunter? Go figure."

"Not to worry. He'll still be there to shadow you, and to do the heavy lifting." Eric puts a finger to his lips. "Should you run into Varick before you leave, do me a favor and keep your assignment on the QT. He'll be disappointed that he missed out." He shrugs. "He *adores* pasties and G-strings."

"Really?" I feign shock. "I never figured him as the type who loved seeing a naked woman wiggle against a pole!"

"No, no, no, my dear! He loves to *wear* the items, not admire them from afar."

"Duly noted. My lips are sealed."

"Truly a waste," Eric murmurs wistfully. "Jack is a very lucky man."

"Speaking of which, this is my fourth trial. You made me a promise—"

He holds up a finger to silence me. "Have you forgotten that you reprimanded me in front of my underlings? Do you realize how deeply you hurt me?" He pats his heart—well, the place in the chest where it would be, if he had one. Noting my frown, he shrugs. "My dear Mrs. Craig, after this mission, I'll decide if your cruelness merits my forgiveness and your husband's return."

He turns me around and pats my rump *adieu*.

My assignment's shadow, Gunter, smirks when he sees this.

I guess he'll see a lot more of me when we reach the Coyote Cabaret.

How I'd love to slip him a mickey! But I have to keep my eyes on the prize: bringing Jack home.

I'll use the mickey on Chen instead.

WANG CHEN IS SMITTEN—UNFORTUNATELY, NOT WITH ME.

That's not to say I don't have my own set of admirers. Despite the number of dollar bills stuck in my G-string by truck drivers taking time off their cross-country treks, Arizona State students coming off exams, or golfers who just want to forget their mulligans, I only have eyes for the Chinese scientist at the end of the Coyote Cabaret's bar, who is nursing his whiskey sour as he waits for the girl of his dreams to take the stage: a long-legged redhead called Misty Lake.

As it pertains to originality, my own nom de plum, Honey Graham, leaves a lot to be desired. But at this very moment, that's not my biggest worry. I've got to figure out how to steal Chen's affections.

"Don't worry," Dominic murmurs in my earbud. "I've got it covered. Just be there to commiserate with him when the time is right."

An upbeat tempo announces Misty's arrival on center stage. Admittedly, her gyrations are mesmerizing. I take note of a few moves that might win me major brownie points, should my honeymoon ever get back on track.

Hell yeah it will!

Dominic's college professor attire, which includes a

tweed jacket with elbow patches and Harry Potteresque-rimmed glasses, easily attracts his fair share of lap dancers—or maybe it's the number of ten spots he's stuffing inside Misty's tasseled bra.

Ten minutes later, Chen, who can't seem to keep up with the auction for her attentions, gives up in frustration.

That's when I make my move. Sidling over, I nod toward one of the private rooms. "I know just how to make you feel better." I lick my lips slowly as I add, "And it's on the house."

His eyes open wide at the thought.

I pick up his drink and beckon him to follow me into the empty room. Even before he crosses the threshold, I've dropped a liquid roofie into his glass.

As I start my bump-and-grind routine, I encourage him to take a sip. Instead, he cops a feel.

When I slap his hand away, the drink spills onto the already sticky floor.

Not good.

There's a knock on the back door. Oh hell, Gunter is already here with the van.

He doesn't wait for me to open it, but comes barging in. When Chen sees the gun in his hand, he looks over at me, "You already called a bouncer?"

"Come with me," Gunter growls.

Chen decides to throw a chair at his head instead.

Dodging it, Gunter slams into the wall. The gun is knocked out of his hand. Chen sails past him and into the parking lot.

"Donna, go after him," Ryan shouts in my ear. "Convince him to play along. Otherwise, we lose Jack."

I scoop up the gun as I run out the door.

Chen is bobbing and weaving across the parking lot. When I can take a clean shot, I aim for his leg but hit a car tire instead. Luckily, my next shot gets him in the thigh.

He writhes in pain.

I get to him just as Gunter stumbles to the van. Before he can drive it over to us, I slap Chen in the face and hiss, "Play along, or he'll kill you. He doesn't know it, but once you're on the plane you'll be taken into Witness Protection. Understand?"

He groans as he nods.

Gunter skids to a stop in front of him. As I help him load Chen into the back of the van, the video of Jack's kidnapping comes to mind.

The plane and the Chinese pilot waiting for Chen at Scottsdale Airport are Acme assets. After Gunter and I wave goodbye, it'll land in Los Angeles, not Beijing. Instead, a Gulfstream-sized drone with its Black Box containing a pre-recorded May Day message will fly the route that was to be taken by Chen's private plane—

Only to lose steam somewhere over the Pacific.

Eric will be in the clear, since the Chinese pilot whose job it was to fly Chen back to Beijing will take the blame for miscalculating their fuel needs. In truth, he'll be granted asylum here in the United States, and put into Witness Protection.

So will Chen, if he can jog his photographic memory

regarding any Chinese state secrets that he may have seen.

So you see, all's well that end's well—

If it also accomplishes the goal of bringing Jack home to me.

12

Jack's Diary, Day 6

Dear Donna,

I am finally being treated like a human being. But as I suspected, my upward mobility comes with a very steep price. Let me explain:

Since killing Oscar and Big Boy, apparently, I now have a new role in the palace: that of El Maestro's official enforcer.

Today, when I was released into the prison yard—always at nine in the morning, sharp—the other prisoners grew silent and backed away.

It wasn't as if I chose this role for myself, or for that matter, my victims. In fact, they were already chosen for me, by El Maestro: not just one but two prisoners each day.

My first challenger did not seem shocked at all when El Maestro called out his name. In fact, it was as if he'd already prepared himself for his fate: not just in the way he stood by himself while most of the other prisoners clustered in groups with their backs turned to him.

He was a pariah.

As if to counter this reality, he was absorbed in the book he held in his hands. The title was in English: *A Tale of Two Cities*, by Charles Dickens.

The man was in his early thirties: tall with a sinewy build, and he wore glasses. Although his prison garb was just as dingy with dirt and sweat as everyone else's in this godforsaken place, he wore it without disgrace, as if it were a badge of honor.

Is there nobility in taking your last breath in the prison yard of a drug king?

Personally, I didn't want to find out. When it came down to his life or mine, his alleged crime against one of the most notorious men in Mexico didn't matter. The only thing I cared about was living yet one more day in the hope of getting home to you.

"You've each been given a gun containing a single bullet," El Maestro declared. "On my count to three, you will shoot to kill, *hombres*." He paused to make his point, then added, "The one who does so lives to see another day. However, if your conscience causes you to miss, let me assure you that my guards feel no such burden."

My opponent met my stare with a smile.

"Uno…Dos…Tres!"

Still, I paused just long enough to let my opponent take the first shot.

He swung his gun up and around: not at me, but in El Maestro's direction.

Our host's eyes widened with fear.

My opponent's shot went off.

He missed.

He dropped his head in resignation of his fate and faced me.

When my single bullet entered his heart, it was my hope that this brave man saw it as a blessing.

His body had already crumpled to the ground by the time the guards' bullets spewed from their guns.

EL MAESTRO'S FURY AT THIS UNEXPECTED TURN OF EVENTS was demonstrated in his next death match choice: a *narco* lieutenant from another gang.

He was the man who had been in the hellhole before me; the one who left behind a steaming pile of shit as a present.

"The *hombre*'s name is Eduardo Conseco. His boss, El Martillo, is El Maestro's sworn enemy," Jaime explained to me. "He has not broken his silence as to the location of his boss's closest safe house. It is time for him to pay the piper: you."

This time, the other prisoners formed a circle of

humanity—or I should say inhumanity, considering how the bets were flying fast and furiously around us.

We were jostled to opposite sides of the yard. A guard came out with odd weapons: a double-sided hatchet was put halfway between us on my left, and a bow and arrow, an equal distance away, on my right.

From his balcony perch, El Maestro proclaimed loudly, "When I drop my bandana, you will choose your weapon of choice, and fight to the death."

I have to think fast. The hatchet would allow me to do a lot of damage, but only if I were up close to my target. The bow and arrow would keep him far away. But I'd have to work fast, and the quiver held only three arrows.

If he'd never used a bow and arrow, his instincts would send him to the hatchet. As you know, Donna, I've used both.

Even before the bandana made it to the ground, Eduardo was off and running—

As I suspected, toward the hatchet.

I took off in the opposite direction. I had no time to lose.

EDUARDO KNEW WHAT HE HAD TO DO: GET UP CLOSE AND personal—and fast.

My goal was to keep him away, which meant delivering a kill shot before he was within striking distance.

At one hundred yards, he dodged my first arrow, if

only by an inch. Exhilarated, he came at me even faster, roaring like a bull.

At fifty yards, he ducked just in time so that my second arrow soared over his head.

His pause gave me the time I needed to place my last arrow.

But this time, I waited until he was only twenty feet away before drawing the bowstring and releasing the arrow—

It pierced his heart.

He had enough momentum to keep moving even after the light left his eyes.

He fell face down at my feet with such a force that the hatchet's blade creased the ground.

El Maestro clapped to show his pleasure at the outcome. The murmurs from the prisoners rose to a fevered buzz.

Jaime was still trying to pull it out when I walked off.

El Maestro called to one of his bodyguards. The man listened to his instructions, then hurried off the balcony.

A moment later he was in the prison yard, giving instructions to Jaime.

This time, my escort prodded me across the plaza through a side door on a different side of El Maestro's palace.

"The first man," I mutter to Jaime, "Who was he?"

"Just another *narco,*" he assures me. "I pray that someday they will all kill each other and leave the rest of my countrymen in peace."

WE WENT DOWN A LONG HALLWAY, PASSING SEVERAL PEOPLE in lab coats.

A strange smell hit me straight on: vinegar.

One-Eyed Juan was right. There is a meth lab on the premises.

The odor seeped out of a room on the right. The room had a glass window to the hall, allowing someone—El Maestro, I presume—to keep an eye on the action taking place inside.

Instinctively, I turned my head toward it. The drapes on the window were drawn.

Jaime tapped me with his rifle. "Eyes straight ahead, *Gringo.*"

The hallway ended at a door with a window covered in bars, but it opened into a much larger room, with a real bed, not just a cot. It also had a couple of straight back chairs, and a padded table that was hip high. On the wall across from the table was a large mirror. I'd no doubt it had two-way capabilities, so that my guards could monitor my movements.

The room also had a window to the prisoners' yard, but it was high on the wall, narrow in its height, and had bars.

When I entered, I found I was not alone. A woman in her mid-twenties stood before me. She had on a flowing white cotton shift. In the narrow shaft of light coming in through the window, it was obvious that she wore nothing under it.

I'd be lying if I told you she wasn't pretty: long dark hair, high cheekbones, and ample breasts despite slim hips.

In other words, the kind of beauty that can stop men in their tracks.

But there was much sadness in her cat-like eyes.

Is that what I'm supposed to do too? I wondered. Are they using her as bait? As a reward?

Too bad, it ain't happening.

There was a crate on a nearby bench. It held several jars. Each was filled with a lotion, each lotion a different color. "What is that?" I asked in English.

"Salves, to heal you." She pointed to the padded bench.

"Is that why you're here, to make me feel better?" Even if her English wasn't that good, she heard the taunting tone in my voice.

"Y—yes," she stuttered. She bowed her head. "My name is Lola. I am...I am yours to do with, as you please."

Not very convincing. Then again, she had nothing to prove to me. But obviously, someone was waiting for my answer. My guess was *El Maestro*.

I knew what he wanted. I also knew I wasn't going to fall for it.

"Sit, *por favor*," she begged me.

I stood for the longest time. Finally, I shrugged and did as she asked.

She waited until I was seated, then opened the smallest of the jars. It was filled with a thick green cream. She stood before me, scanning my body. The worst of my many cuts caught her attention: a deep one, on my left side.

She nodded at it.

Grudgingly, I nodded back.

Slowly, she moved toward me. Her touch was gentle, but the cream was anything but. At first it felt cold, but then it burned as it worked its way into the wound.

Then, as if by magic, it seemed to heal.

She moved around my body, eyeing each injury, dabbing the deepest with the salve, or patting the bruises with a fragrant dark lotion.

Relieved from the pain, I relaxed. I closed my eyes.

"You can lie down if you wish." Her fingers pressed on a bruise in the center of my back.

I obliged her.

I felt her hands massage the spot with her thumbs, then her knuckles. I let loose with an involuntary groan as pleasure took the place of the pain.

She hesitated a mere second.

Just then, I opened my eyes. I saw her in the mirror. A slim knife was cupped in the palm of her hand.

She was here to kill me.

Just as her hand raised the knife to stab me in my back, I turned around and grabbed her arm by the wrist and slammed her arm down onto the table beside me. In another second, I'd twisted her arm back behind her.

Lola grunted as she struggled, but I yanked her toward me, so close that we were face to face.

She shook so hard that I felt I would break her. Her eyes opened wide with terror.

"Why did El Maestro choose you?" I asked.

The truth came out in a spitting hiss. "Your first victim today—Miguel Ramírez—was my...*cómo se dice*...how do you say?" She closes her eyes, as if doing so will help her see the word in her mind's eye. "My fiancé. He was *un profesor! He defied El Maestro!* He rallied his *estudiantes* to do so as well!"

"But a guard told me he was a drug peddler." Shit.

"And you believed him?" She smirked at my naiveté. "Only two of the men you've killed so far were *El Maestro's* competitors. The others defied him! They wanted him to die, so that we could break free of the drugs that tear our country apart." She wiped away a tear. "But, unlike Miguel, they are afraid to speak out, let alone overtake his army. And now Miguel is dead because of you."

"I'm sorry. Had I known..." My voice trailed off.

"Had you known, then what? Would you have let him live? Would you have sacrificed yourself for him?"

No. We both knew it.

She read it in my sigh. "Like you, I wish he'd been a better shot," I muttered.

Limp and defeated, she crumpled into my arms. "*Todo está perdido,*" she whispered.

All is lost.

"*Nunca,*" I vowed. Never.

This one word calmed her. Tears ran down her face as she awakened to the harsh reality of her true dilemma. "I have failed to seduce you, and I have failed to kill you. When I leave this room, El Maestro will do both to me."

I wiped the dampness from her face. "And you believe him? Perhaps he wanted you to kill me."

"No!" She shook her head adamantly. "Had he known I would even try, he would not have sent me as your prize. But now…" she blushed. "He will take my virginity. He will make me his *puta*—his whore."

"Why would he feel the need to reward me with the… honor? My God, he must know I paused just long enough for Miguel to make that shot."

"His ego would never let him believe it. He told me that if I'm to stay alive, I must please you. I am your prize —to encourage you to stay strong because you are his new '*verdugo.*'" Noting my confused look, she tried again: "His new executioner."

I almost laughed out loud. "Is that what I am?"

"*Sí!* You are now a legend! No one has fought so many for so long! The longer you are victorious, the more money he makes." Her frown was so quick and so slight that I doubted my room's hidden camera had time to pick up on it. "The other *narcos* are now sending their strongest prisoners to fight *El Santo*. They call them *los gladiadores.*"

"Gladiators, eh?" My laugh made her shudder. She thought I was a mad man. Hell, maybe I was. Why else would I have muttered, "Help me escape."

"*Si*…but you must take me with you." It wasn't a plea or a question. It was a declaration.

"Deal." I needed her to survive.

And she needed me.

I whispered in her ear, "Play along with what I say." Then, loudly, for anyone else listening in, I declared, "Lola, I will fight with all my might, as long as you are here to visit me every day. It is not just your potions that make me stronger, but your beauty and your kindness."

I released her, but she held on for dear life. "El Santo," she stated, loudly and proudly.

"I am anything but a saint I assure you. Otherwise, Miguel would be here with you," I muttered.

Lola shook her head sadly. "Miguel would not have survived prison," she murmured softly. "And it would have broken his heart to see what El Maestro will do to me if we fail."

Donna, should I fall, I pray you never know the truth of what happened to me.

13

Communication Issues

Hubbies, it's almost as if your wives speak a different language, isn't it? Let me translate for you:

When she says: "Sure, go ahead. You certainly don't need my permission…"

What she really means is: "If you do, I'll cold-shoulder you until you're blue in the face from begging my forgiveness."

When she says: "Someone called here looking for you, but she didn't leave her name."

What she really means is: "If you're whoring around on me, my lawyer will take you for every dollar you have and half of what you will earn for the rest of your life. Time to tell your tart to take a walk."

And, finally, when she makes the request: "Please don't do that anymore."

What she really means is: "If you do that again, this cleaver will go flying toward your head."

The language of love is the easiest of all to understand. Ain't it grand?

As pleased as Eric was with the outcome of my last trial, I presume he'll grant me the favor of allowing me to call home and check on my children.

I walk over to the door of his study, only to find it closed. I'm just about to knock when I hear his voice. It is raised in anger. He's having a fight with someone, but the door is so thick that all I can make out is, "That wasn't our agreement, señor! I told you to keep him in solitary—not to throw him in with your den of killers in some sort of—of blood sport! …Unacceptable! I'm not one of your kingpin pinheads with no true appreciation for life, let alone an asset's unique skills! El Maestro…El Maestro, *silencio!* You'll do as I say, or I'll—"

"It's not polite to snoop," Varick's singsong taunt sends his hot breath into my ear, giving me the shivers.

Faking innocence, I flutter my lashes even as I pout. "You're not going to tell on me, are you?"

He rolls his eyes in contemplation. "Depends. What was he saying?"

"Oh, I dunno. These doors and walls are pretty thick."

"Ya think? Let's test one." He slams me up against the

wall by putting an arm across my chest. The next thing I know, his tongue is darting down my throat.

Yuck.

I bite down hard.

Hearing his yelp, Eric opens the door. He scowls when he sees us standing there, and covers the phone receiver with his hand. Ignoring me, he jerks the thumb of his other hand at Varick.

I stick my foot in the door before he can close it on my face. "I want to call my children. They need to hear from me."

Eric's growl is loud enough to hear in the other room. "Hugo! Escort Mrs. Craig to her room. She's allowed one phone call, to her children. Dial it for her, and wait until you hear a child's voice."

They close the door behind them.

The good news: it'll be a while before Varick can talk, let alone squeal on me.

The bad news: once he does, Eric will want to know what I heard.

Obviously, it wasn't enough because it doesn't make any sense to me.

Hugo is Johnny-on-the-spot. Eric's little toady strong-arms me back to my room and locks me in it while he goes off to parts unknown to retrieve my cellphone.

"Emma, do me a favor and see if you can pull up anything on the name 'El Maestro.' It might be a Spanish code name."

"On it," she murmurs.

Just then, Hugo comes in with my cellphone. "Thank you," I say sweetly.

In unison, Emma and Hugo answer, "You're welcome," albeit Hugo's gruff reply indicates that he's somewhat suspicious of my kindness.

That's what he gets for eavesdropping.

"Mom's on the phone!" Jeff's shout reverberates through my cellphone, and possibly through all of Hilldale as well.

Just hearing his voice makes me tear up. "Tell me about your week," I implore him.

"I was the starting pitcher in the two games you and Dad missed." Yes, there is a tinge of melancholy in his voice. "The last one was a no-hitter—"

"Let me speak to Mommy," Trisha begs. "Please, please, please! I'll let you have my second piece of chocolate cake!"

I sigh. "Aunt Phyllis is allowing you to have *two* pieces of cake?"

"Let me put you on speaker," Jeff suggests. "You can yell at her instead of us."

"Great, please do." How I long to hear my sweet aunt's voice.

"Don't listen to a word they say!" Aunt Phyllis warns me. "They begged, and I caved."

"She's fibbing," Evan calls out from the background.

"She's trying to buy our good behavior."

"A lot of good all this cake is doing for that goal," she retorts.

"Mom, why haven't you guys sent us any selfies?" Mary asks.

"We've…we've been doing other stuff." I try to keep from choking on my lie.

"I'll bet!" Jeff makes kissing sounds. Then: "Ouch! Evan smacked me in the back of my head!"

"Good, because someone needs to smack some manners into you," Aunt Phyllis pipes up.

"By the way," Mary buts in, "Babs wants to know if I can sleep over at her place tomorrow night. She asked Wendy's mom, too—"

"I'd prefer you stay home." If I could, I'd never let any of my loved ones out of my sight. "Tell you what: why don't you see if their moms will allow them to sleep over at our place instead?"

"All-right!" Aunt Phyllis crows. "Par-TAY!"

"Then I guess you wouldn't mind if I have a few of the guys from my lacrosse team stop by too—" Evan declares.

"Not at all," I counter, "as long as they do so *tonight*, as opposed to tomorrow evening. It's not going to be *that* kind of sleepover, understood, young man?"

Evan sighs. "Yeah, okay."

"Am I right, Aunt Phyllis?"

"Yeah." She sounds even more disappointed than him. Under her breath, she mutters, "Party pooper."

"Mommy, where's Daddy?" Trisha asks. "Can we speak to him?"

I stay silent for so long that soon the kids are asking if I'm still on the line.

"Yes, yes, I'm here! He's…he's still on the beach. Had he known I'd be so lonely that I'd need to call you, I'm sure he would have come inside too."

"Can't you go get him for us? Please? Pretty please—"

"Mom, are you and Dad going to be home in time for my next game?" Jeff interrupts. "It's the day after tomorrow, at four o'clock."

"We'll…we'll certainly try." *No tears! Change the topic…*

Mary does it for me. Admittedly, it's just as sobering. "Hey Mom, did you hear about Daniel Parker's death? Right on the red carpet, for the latest *Lorne* movie! How could that happen? He was so young!—"

Hugo gives me the high sign. Eric is off the phone, and wants to discuss my assignment for tomorrow.

My good-byes are filled with instructions: Listen to your aunt, feed the dogs, and no boys at the sleepover.

As I hang up, Trisha is sobbing over how much she misses me.

Oh, my sweet baby, the feeling is mutual.

If this is how empty I feel just saying goodbye on the phone, I wonder if I'll be able to keep it together should the dreaded day comes in which I have to tell them that Jack is dead.

～

WHEN I GET OFF THE PHONE, ERIC SUMMONS ME TO HIS study—presumably to chastise me for eavesdropping.

Instead, I'm met with one of his broad benign smiles. "I'm sure that you're aware of the fact that your very dear friend, President Chiffray, is still here in California for a supposedly private summit with a few of his closest Middle Eastern friends."

Eric's reminder turns my blood cold. "It's why you're here in the first place, isn't it? And why you planted Eileen and Frannie in the White House?" I retort.

"Yes, well, now that both of my colleagues were cut down in the prime of their lives—thanks to you, if not exactly by your hand—a little restitution is in order, don't you think?"

"How, exactly?"

"I need you to retrieve something from Eileen's desk within the walls of Lion's Lair."

"That's impossible! In the first place, no unauthorized personnel are being allowed in or out of Lion's Lair while the summit is in progress. And secondly, I'm supposed to be on my honeymoon. Both POTUS and FLOTUS know that! They were at my wedding, or have you forgotten?"

"No, my pet, I haven't. And it also has not slipped my mind that your esteemed president has a deep and sincere affection for you." Eric's hand grazes my shoulder with a gentle wistfulness.

I can barely quell my sudden urge to wrench his arm out of its socket.

Think. Of. Jack...

I take a deep breath before speaking. "What is your ridiculous plan to get me into Lion's Lair?"

"It's quite simple. Tell the president's aide—what is his name again? Oh yes, Todd Courtland—that you've come to retrieve something you lost in Lee's office, and you just now remembered Eileen mentioning that she'd found it. This, in fact."

He holds up my antique necklace—an heirloom handed down to me by my mother. Not only had I worn it during the births of each of my children, it hung on my neck during my wedding ceremony.

He must have stolen it out of my suitcase while I was doing his bidding these past few days.

I snatch it out of his hand. "How dare you!"

"Please, Mrs. Craig, calm down."

"I'm losing patience with your little games! This will be my fifth trial. You promised I'd have Jack after four."

"This isn't a game! Surely you know I'd use everything at my disposal to infiltrate the summit"—he leans in and hisses—"just as you'll do everything it takes to bring your husband home, safe and sound."

He knows I can't argue with that.

My silence earns me a nod. "You'll plant it in the top left drawer of Ms. Woodley's desk. It gives you the excuse you need to open the drawer, where you will also retrieve a small pale blue envelope, which you will bring back to me."

"Why? What does it contain?"

He chuckles. "The secrets of the universe, of course!

Now, get going. Gunter is bringing around the town car as we speak."

"Gunter—again? Ack! He's <u>such</u> a bore! Why can't Varick drive me? That way, if we get stuck on the 405, at least he can bring me up to speed on the latest fashion trends."

"Varick is busy running a little errand for me." He shrugs as if it is of no importance.

"We haven't been thrown together to amuse each other, Donna. You know that as well as me. Let's not pretend otherwise. Otherwise, one of us will live to regret it."

His way of showing me that I'm dismissed is to turn and face the window.

Works for me, asshole.

I saunter out, as if the decision to go was mine all along. If I could, I'd run out of there.

Gunter stands outside my bedroom door while I change into something fitting for my unexpected visit to Lion's Lair: nothing too fancy; a little black dress will do.

I wait until I've entered my bathroom and turned on the faucet before asking Ryan, "Did you hear all that?"

"Yes," Ryan murmurs into my ear. "I'm sure that NSA operatives have already scrubbed Eileen's desk from top to bottom."

"Would a simple sealed envelope have drawn their attention?" I ask.

"Possibly. If not and it's still there, I'll have it retrieved and assessed. In fact, Arnie is on his way there now." He hesitates, then adds, "I'll also inform POTUS of your itinerary, so that he's prepared."

"Not too prepared, I hope," I warn him. "It's got to look like a surprise. Otherwise, Gunter will be suspicious, not to mention we don't know if there are other Quorum operatives embedded there." I'm specifically referring to Babette, and he knows it.

"Duly noted," Ryan promises. "If the envelope is there, you'll have to hand it off to Arnie, so that any needed analysis of its intel can be done on the fly by Arnie and Emma—that is before you turn it over to Eric."

"Is that even possible?" I wonder.

"Depends on what it is. If it's a thumb drive, a microdot, even a slip of paper with an encrypted message —if they can hack it, they'll then scrub the data, and perhaps plant false intel."

"A little payback?"

"Exactly. In any event, they'll come prepared."

"We're already on our way to Lion's Lair," Emma assures us. "You know, I'll bet Varick is going to retrieve Jack."

I pray she's right. Still, I have to ask: "Why do you say that?"

"Because of the angry conversation he was having on the phone with this El Maestro person just before Varick caught you listening outside his door. And now he's got Varick going who knows where—"

"It's a possible lead," Ryan concedes. "Don't worry, Donna. Abu will be driving the limousine summoned to pick up Varick. I'll have him plant a tracer on him. That way, if he's anywhere near Jack, we'll be there when he needs us."

Yes, Jack needs us.

He needs *me*.

All the more reason why my assignment must succeed.

Apparently, Ryan feels the same way. "In fact, Abu will shadow Varick to his final destination."

Maybe by the time I come back, Jack will be here too.

As is the West Coast White House's protocol, Gunter and I are stopped at the guard station at the base of Lion's Lair's private road. The mention of my name elicits raised brows from the guards. Obviously, my reputation precedes me.

It also causes them to search the trunk of the car, and to scrutinize Gunter more closely.

He scowls back at them. Should his ugly mug already be in the NSA's facial recognition program, I may have to duck and cover when the bullets go flying.

But no, he merits no more than a shrug. Apparently,

Eileen was successful in keeping her Quorum associates under the radar because we're waved through the gate.

The climb to the top of Hilldale's largest peak is a good five minutes. As we near Lion's Lair, I look down the hill. Spotting my house, I blow it a kiss. I wish the children had been outside. I would have loved to see them.

Who knows when the next time will be?

I'm sure Jack feels the same way.

The guard at the grand estate's second entry post gives us a cursory glance before waving us up to the circular driveway, where we are met by yet another phalanx of Secret Service agents.

No doubt, the discovery that the president's personal secretary and his daughter's nanny were spies—just one day prior to the Middle East summit—has kept everyone on high alert.

My car door is opened by one of the detail. But before Gunter can get out of the car, an agent places both hands on the door. "Mrs. Craig has clearance, not you."

While Gunter fumes, I run up the steps.

Todd Courtland, one of Lee's administration's aides, meets me at the threshold. He also happens to be POTUS's liaison to the National Security Council. "Donna? Well, isn't this a welcome surprise!" He clasps my hands in his. "I'd thought you'd still be on your honeymoon."

"I'm here to pick up something I left in...in Lee's office."

"Oh?" Todd frowns as he takes a quick glance at his watch. "He's tied up right now in a very important meeting—"

"I'll only be a minute. Truly, you don't have to disturb him—"

"The way he feels about you? I'd be fired if I didn't." I don't like the way he gives me the once-over. "Follow me. You can wait in Eileen's—I mean, the outer office."

As we head down the hall, I ask, "Has the president found a replacement for her?"

Todd rolls his eyes. "Not yet. As you can imagine, her —let's just call it her untimely demise—came at a very inopportune time. I've picked up some of the slack, but for lack of a better term, Eileen knew where all the bodies were buried."

And buried a few too. I was almost one of them.

A moment later, we're in the late secretary's office and I stand by the desk while he knocks on Lee's door.

No answer.

"Ah, well." He shrugs. "The president and his guests were supposed to take a break right about now, but you know how these things can be."

"Long-winded, to say the least."

He chuckles. "That's putting it mildly. He must still be tied up. Let me check the grand salon to see where they stand."

I wait until he's at least fifty feet down the hall before moving to the back of Eileen's desk.

The top left drawer opens without a problem. It

contains the usual office supplies: pens, a letter opener, scissors, paper clips, pads, a bottle of White-Out, but nothing that looks like a small blue envelope.

I tug the drawer so that it opens even more so that I can place my hand all the way to the back—

Ah, here it is.

It's just large enough for a greeting card, and just as slim, which tells me it holds nothing more than a piece of paper.

I've just slipped it into the pocket of my dress when I hear him say, "Donna?"

I turn around to face Lee.

By the time he walks over to me, I can extend my hand forward.

He takes it, not to shake, but to hold, as old friends do.

He strokes it gently with his thumb, not as an old friend, but as an adoring admirer.

He doesn't drop it when he hears Todd exclaim, "Oh… Mr. President! Here you are. I went to find you so that I could tell you that Mrs. Craig is here."

"Mrs. Craig…" The reminder of my marital status darkens the gleam in Lee's eyes. "Thanks, Todd." He dismisses his aide with a wave of his hand. "We'll be in my office. Make sure our other guests have everything they need."

Lee never lets go of my hand. Instead he takes it to steer me into the private office, and closes the door.

The smirk on Todd's face should shame me, but it

doesn't. I mean, why should it? Lee and I have never been intimate. We're merely friends.

We both know it, although Lee has yet to admit it to himself.

~

LEE SAYS NOTHING. INSTEAD, HE STARES DOWN AT ME.

When he lets go of my hand, it's to embrace me. "I'm sorry about Jack," he whispers.

That does it. The dam breaks and my tears flood my eyes before cascading down my cheeks and into my mouth, where I'm babbling on about how worried I am for him, and how scared I am that he'll never come home to us, and how much I miss him and need to feel him next to me.

He holds me as if he doesn't ever want to let me go. "Donna, anything you need—for you and for Jack—it's at your disposal. All you have to do is ask. If you want me to have the CIA grab Eric for extraordinary rendition—"

"Thanks, Lee. I appreciate it." I nod as I gulp down my sobs. "But we can't now—at least, not until we know where Jack is, and can get him to safety. For all we know, Eric has ordered his captors to expect timely check-in calls. If he doesn't make it—"

The thought that the call will never come brings even more tears.

This time, Lee's lips graze my cheeks—first one, then the other—as if willing my tears away.

He has to stop. He must know this too. But because he doesn't, I start to say something—

Just as his lips slide to mine.

"Talk about a short honeymoon." The sound of Babette's voice has the opposite effect on Lee, causing his hands to drop to his sides, and his eyes to turn to steel.

She moves closer. "Don't mind Lee, Donna. My morning sickness has put him in heat. Unfortunately for him, after all this country has been through, the last thing it needs is a president with a wandering eye. Quite pathetic, don't you think?"

I take a step back. "Lee was just comforting me about…a family matter."

She chortles mirthlessly. "Isn't that Jack's job?" She glances around the room. "Where is he, anyway?"

I stare at her, waiting for some subliminal clue that she already knows the answer to that.

Lee doesn't have my patience. He jerks her by the arm toward the door. "Our guests are waiting for us, dear."

Her glare never leaves me. "What…we're supposed to leave her here, in your private office, all by her little lonesome? Why, aren't you a trusting soul!"

"Unlike you, she's earned it."

A slap could not have hurt her more. His retort brings tears to her eyes.

She wrenches her arm from his hand.

The click of her heels reverberates like shotgun blasts as she runs down the hall.

Angered and shamed, Lee drops his head.

When I take my leave, I kiss his cheek.

"WHERE ARE YOU GUYS?" I WHISPER.

"I'm in the catering van outside the kitchen door," Emma replies. "I've tapped into the security cams."

"And I'm…I'm…right behind you!" Arnie sounds out of breath. He also sounds as if he's walking on his hands and knees.

I glance down the long hallway. Nope, nobody there. "I'm almost at the front door," I warn him.

"And I'm almost…!" As Arnie slams his fist into something metallic, it echoes in my ear. "Damn! Dead end!"

I sigh. "Seriously, dude, where are you?"

I hear a clatter behind the door to my right.

I glance around. No one is watching, so I open it—

Just in time to see Arnie climbing down from a ceiling vent inside this little janitorial closet. At least he's dressed like Lee's Secret Service detail: white shirts, black suits and ties, obviously ear pieces and a firearm bulge in the right place: his right side, at the waist.

"Really, Arnie? That's the best you can do?" I slap my forehead to tamp down the urge to throttle him.

"Since this Middle Eastern summit started, this place has more security than the White House! Hell, I should know. I've busted into there, too."

Whatever. I hand over the envelope. "Get cracking."

The flap on the envelope is folded under, so it opens

easily. Arnie lifts it open. As I suspected, the only thing it contains is a measly slip of paper: white, with two rows of numbers typed on it.

"Damn it!" he mutters.

"*Shhhh!*" I put my hand over his mouth. Thank goodness the walls are four inches thick in this place. "What's that supposed to mean?"

"I was hoping for a delivery method of some sort—you know, a microdot, or a thumb drive."

"Why? What difference does it make?"

"See this top line of numbers? It tells us the location of the intel: apparently some digital cloud. If this had held the intel, all I'd have to worry about is hacking it. Oh, well." He holds it up to the light. "There are no watermarks, and no fairy dust. That helps." Next, he pulls out his iPad and scans the paper to make a jpeg of the encryption before handing it back to me. I start to open the door, but he pulls me back. "Don't leave yet for the city. That way, you buy me time to hack this baby—"

"Donna! Arnie! A housekeeper is headed your way!" Emma hisses in our ears.

There's nowhere to hide.

The doorknob jiggles, then there's a pause. The next thing we hear is the tinkling of keys.

I grab Arnie's face between my hands and plant my lips on his kisser.

"*Oh!*"

We break apart to find that the housekeeper's eyes are

open wide in alarm. Rattled, she takes few steps back into the hall and slams the door.

When I turn to Arnie. His face is bright red. "I...um...I think we better get out of here."

"I agree!" Emma doesn't sound too happy. "And you two lovebirds better hurry. The housekeeper is talking to one of POTUS's Secret Service detail. I'd hate for Arnie to end up in some penitentiary for breaking and entering, let alone for impersonating an officer of the law. His roomie may want to do more than steal a 'kiss.'"

While Arnie sputters out an apology to his wife, I duck out the door.

Gunter is exactly where I left him: cooling his heels beside the limo. I snap my fingers at him so that he can open my door like a proper chauffeur.

He practically pulls it off its hinge. After I slide in, he slams it shut.

We have pulled out of Hilldale and inched onto the 405 when I realize I'm missing something.

"Arnie! You have the envelope," I mutter under my breath.

I hear a screech of wheels and honking horns. "Oh, shit!" Arnie moans. "You're right. Okay, we skipped our exit so that we can follow you to the Montage. Before we get there, we'll figure out a way to hand it off to you there."

"That's only half my problem," I hiss through gritted teeth. "You've still got to tell us what's in it."

"Tell me something I don't already know, okay?" Arnie's voice gets high and squeaky when he's scared.

"Just keep working it, baby," Emma coos. "It's the 405. You've got plenty of time."

For once, I thank providence for LA traffic.

"GOT IT!" ARNIE'S WHOOP RINGS THROUGH MY EAR. I CLOSE my eyes from the pain throbbing behind them.

Gunter looks at me through the rearview mirror. "Did you say something?"

"Just that I think your driving is superb."

His frown deepens.

"You need to learn how to take a compliment," I scold him.

"Donna, here's the deal." Ryan's calm determination brings me back down to my deadly reality. "Apparently, Eileen has hidden audio feeds in Lee's office, as well as in the conference rooms."

"In other words, she was recording U.S. state secrets so that the Quorum can sell them to our enemies," Emma points out.

"Exactly," Ryan replies. "I presume these Middle East talks will soon find their way into the hands of ISIL, which will endanger the success of our military efforts in the region." He sighs. "I've informed POTUS of the breech. He's authorized the immediate destruction of all data in the cloud. And to keep the Quorum and its clients in the dark, Acme has already started the process of producing audio playback that should have them moving their cells right into the hands of our allied troops in the region."

"But first things first," Arnie mutters. "We've got to get this envelope back to Donna. Unfortunately, we're pulling up to the Montage now."

"I've got an idea," Emma declares. "Donna, we'll follow you and Gunter into the elevator. Arnie, when I pinch you, pass the envelope to Donna.

"You're pinching me?" Arnie is miffed. "But...you know I *hate* that! Let me guess: you're getting back at me for kissing Donna—"

"Oh, get real!" Emma retorts. "Although I should point out that you seemed to enjoy it—"

By the time Gunter pulls to the curb, I'm ready to get out.

I STROLL TO THE ELEVATOR AS IF I HAVE ALL THE TIME IN the world.

Gunter doesn't like it. He gets there at least ten seconds before me.

To make him even madder, I stop in front of one of the lobby's gilt mirrors in order to check my lipstick. A bit smudged—from my kiss with Arnie, I guess. No problem. I smack my lips, and smile pretty at my reflection.

By the time I get to the elevator, Emma and Arnie are

on my heels. Arnie has unbuttoned his coat jacket and lost the tie and Secret Service earbud. The way Emma has spiked his hair, he now looks like the casual hipster he's always wanted to be.

Angrily, Gunter slams his fist into the button for our floor: the penthouse level.

Seeing this, Emma giggles.

"Not nice," Arnie reprimands her.

The elevator is rising.

"Ooh, does that make me a bad girl?" she coos.

Arnie looks perplexed. "Um…no…yes? …No, I mean…maybe?"

Through the mirrored doors, Gunter catches her eye.

She winks at him. Who knew she was such a natural?

Certainly not Arnie. His eyes open wide as her hand walks up his gut and over to his right nipple. She tweaks it between her fingers.

Gunter is just as mesmerized as Arnie, especially when Emma pulls him by the neck toward her.

But when her lips meet his, he's the one in control. He slams her up against the elevator so hard that it hops.

She wraps one leg around him, then the other.

Gunter turns to stare, specifically at Emma's hand, which is loosening the top button of her blouse.

Soon, Arnie is helping her.

No better time to pluck the envelope out of Arnie's other hand.

Just in time, too, because the doors open. We've reached our penthouse floor.

Gunter is still staring at them when the doors close shut again.

When I knock, Eric opens the door.

I hand him the envelope. He smiles and honors me with a half bow.

Noting Gunter's absence, he cranes his head down the hall. "What's wrong with him?"

I shrug. "He's busy watching a couple have elevator sex."

"Ah." He nods knowingly. "That's what I get for hiring a eunuch."

____

14

Jack's Diary, Day 7

____

DEAR DONNA,

Word of my death matches has spread throughout the village. Not one to stop the flow of bread and circuses to his people, El Maestro has moved the events out of the prison yard and directly into the town's plaza, which is on the opposite side of his palace.

Today, the villagers gathered several hours before the match, only to be pushed by El Maestro's militia behind the ropes that cordoned off the center of the plaza. In no time, the horde of onlookers stood five or six deep. There was a carnival atmosphere: while the mariachi bands played, children ran around, and vendors sold platters of rice and beans, churros, tamales, sopapillas, and Coca-Cola in the carts placed behind the undulating crowds.

Finally, El Maestro appeared on the balcony of his palace like a feudal lord facing his fiefs. He was flanked by an entourage of AK-47-carrying thugs. He also had a stranger with him: golden blond hair, with piercing blue eyes, clad in a very expensive suit. The look on his face wavered between fascination and disdain.

There was something oddly familiar about him, but I couldn't place it.

El Maestro waited until the throng grew silent before explaining the rules of the game, both in Spanish and in English, the latter I presume was for the benefit of his guest:

The *gringo* was his chosen executioner.

The men I would face had wronged El Maestro. In doing so, they threatened the livelihood and wellbeing of the villagers themselves.

Different weapons would be used in each match.

The game commenced when El Maestro's bandana fell to the floor.

And finally, the match would always end with one competitor's death.

El Maestro's way of channeling Caesar's ancient Rome was to pronounce in a stentorian shout: "Let the games begin!"

The crowd roared its approval.

If my life hadn't depended on it, I would have laughed at the absurdity of this insane spectacle.

My first challenger was a big bull of a man. He

glared at the crowd and waved his fist at them. Then he did the same to me.

"That's Fillipe Abano," Jaime muttered. "He's one bad son of a bitch. He's from the Baja cartel."

"That explains the tan," I murmured back.

Jaime snorted with laughter.

But I wasn't laughing. Neither of us had any doubts as to what would happen in the next few minutes:

Either Fillipe or I would die.

Neither of us intended to be the vanquished.

As part of the pageantry, the guards holding the weapons marched in, side by side, from the palace to the middle of the plaza before one turned left and the other turned right. The weapons left for us were a whip and a spear.

Neither was ideal. If I chose the spear, I'd get one shot to hit or miss.

If I chose the whip, I could disable my opponent to the point where he couldn't throw the spear. On the other hand, I'd have to get close enough to him to do it. Too close, and he'd pierce me easily enough.

Before I could make up my mind, the countdown had begun.

By the time El Maestro's bandana had fallen I was running as fast as I could to the bullwhip—

And so was he.

FILLIPE GOT THERE FIRST.

He scooped it up in a roll and came quickly to his feet.

I kicked a cloud of dust in his face. It sent him gagging and clawing at his eyes with his left hand, but he still got off a quick flick of the whip with his right wrist, gashing my chest. The next lash caught my shoulder.

Enough of this shit, I thought.

I charged right at him, my head bashed into his gut with such force that his feet left the ground until his back smashed into the stucco wall some six feet away.

It was like pinning a spider.

Time to pluck off its legs.

His hand loosened on the whip. I pulled it out of his hand and wrapped it around his neck a few times. It was the perfect leash to drag him a few feet over so that I could pick up the spear.

By the time I stabbed him in the heart, he'd already choked to death. I looked at it like an insurance policy: It never hurts to double up.

El Maestro nodded his approval.

I bowed. The crowd's cheer roared through the plaza in a thunderous wave.

Was it a stroke to my ego, making my name as a killing machine, and impressing one of the most vicious *narcos* in Mexico?

No. I'm just trying to stay alive, Donna. And I have only one thought that feeds all my desires:

Coming home to you.

THE NEXT MAN TO FACE ME WAS A PRIEST.

His eyes were closed and he was kneeling, as in prayer, despite the fact that two guards carried him from under his arms into the plaza. They dumped him onto the ground about fifty feet from me. A moment later, a third guard came into the yard. He was holding two medieval hatchets. He held them up to the crowd so that they might get a good view of the instruments of carnage before he tossed one down in front of each of us.

When El Maestro's bandana fell, I picked up the hatchet.

The priest continued to pray.

I don't know what the man did to anger El Maestro. All I knew was that we were both innocent in this macabre situation. I would not have blamed him in the least had he defended himself. The reality that this holy man was not going to do so—that he was going to let me slaughter him in cold blood, in front of a hushed crowd, many of whom were members of his flock—racked me with guilt.

As I stood over him, I implored him in Spanish, "Padre, please—to live you must fight me."

He opened his eyes to look into mine. "*Hermano*, I do not blame you for your desire to survive. Please, do not blame me for my decision to leave this godforsaken place. By doing so, I serve God's purpose, which is not to lead El Maestro's sheep into an endless state of fear and self-loathing. Should my death at your hand bring the shame they need to right this wrong in their lives, so be it, for it is the will of God."

"You have one last blessing to give." I knelt beside him, and closed my eyes as I bowed my head.

Donna, at that moment, he could have taken his hatchet and chopped off my head. But unlike us, he wasn't a killer.

Unlike us, he celebrated life, first and foremost.

He stood over me and prayed that I would find peace and joy in the life I'd chosen.

Then he dropped to his knees.

I made sure that the cut was swift, if not merciful.

The crowd gasped.

As I knelt again and prayed for my soul, the murmur "El Santo" buzzed through the plaza.

When I opened my eyes, El Maestro and his gringo guest, the blond Adonis, had already left the balcony.

Jaime hustled me back into the palace. When the door closed behind me, I asked, "Why him, Jaime? What did he ever do to El Maestro?"

Jaime put a finger to his lips. His eyes floated upward to a video camera clasped in a corner. I stared at him until he had the guts to say it out loud, if only in a whisper: "He should not have preached against working in the fields."

"The crop they harvest ruins so many lives!"

He shrugged. "They are farmers. No more, no less. As

for those who take heroin, they choose their fate, amigo. If you choose wrong, you lose."

Lola was there, in my room.

She waited until I closed the door and fell across the padded bench before lifting her flowing white cotton skirt high enough so that she could straddle my towel-wrapped waist.

She then wrapped her feet around the outside of my thighs, as if using them as leverage while she warmed her healing lotion in her palms. As she kneaded my upper back, her hands, slick with the lotion, caused her to slide. With each forward stroke, her body rose and fell against mine, while her breasts stroked my back.

Oh, Donna, how I wished they were yours.

She is only playing her part in the illusion we present to guards monitoring the webcam. We imagine them chortling, or perhaps being aroused by our soft porn routine.

In other words, watching our little show while never noticing that we're passing each other information.

I closed my eyes and yawned, as if I were dead to the world. But then, I turned my head to the other side, away from the camera. Gently, I whispered, "Any news?"

Her murmur was slurred, the result of lips that barely moved. "They say that your competitors can no longer see their favorite *putas* until they step up and kill you. *Los gladiadores* are not happy about this, and neither are the women, who have lost their status among their own."

"Anything else?"

"One of the guards heard me call you El Santo—'the Saint.'" Through the mirror, I caught her reflection as she blushed. "So now, it is what the villagers call you. Look! It's right here, in the village newspaper!" She points to the paper she brought in with her, which now lies on the dresser. "Even those who fear that they must fight you pray to you in the hope that you'll give them a swift death." She hesitated before adding, "But those without souls pray that death comes quickly to you, at their hands, so that they may be the next '*verdugo*."

"And what do you pray for, Lola?"

"You have confused him because you refused my advances. He thinks that if he takes me, you may finally lose. Since he bets against your competitors with the other *narcos*, he doesn't want that to happen. I thank *La Virgen Maria* that El Maestro loves money even more than he desires me."

There is no joy in my laughter. When I stop, I mutter, "Eventually, I will lose, Lola. It's inevitable."

Or I'd escape. I must escape, Donna. I must come home to you.

"*Si, Santo*, but you must never let him in on that secret."

"My lips are sealed," I vowed.

15

How Do You Know if He's Strayed?

There are several telltale signs that a husband has been less than faithful. Wives, if his fidelity is important to you, be alert to these signposts:

- *Sign #1: He comes home later and later from work.*
- *Sign #2: He fibs about where he's been, and whom he's been with. (You know this because you followed him after work on several occasions.)*
- *Sign #3: He comes home smelling of another woman's perfume. (And you know who she is!)*
- *Sign #4: He comes home with lipstick on his collar. (And you did not put it there.)*
- *Sign #5: There are nights in which he never comes home at all. (And you know where they are.)*

At this point, your goal should not be finding even more proof, but getting rid of the evidence—

Of his existence that is!

While you're at it, get a good lawyer, because you'll probably need one when they find the bodies.

"MY DEAR, I HAVE A PRESENT FOR YOU!" ERIC'S declaration is made with the joy of a father announcing that the kiddies can now enter the living room in order to ooh and ah at the family Christmas tree.

I'm not a child, which is reason enough to denote my skepticism with silence and a raised brow.

He dabs his lips with his linen napkin. It's become a ritual with us, this tradition of breaking bread after a mission, usually in a unique but out-of-the-way boîte that enjoys a superb reputation amongst the right people.

Tonight, however, we are having dinner in a private room at Scarpetta, in the Montage's lobby. The wait list for reservations is three months long. Even then, it's a lottery as to what night you'll be served.

Eric has a standing reservation for any night he wants.

The menu is eclectic. Mushroom papillote with truffle. Sea urchin in a Ibérico-pork broth. An herbal salad served in a fried pig's ear. Foie gras ice cream.

Eric keeps these dinners cozy, just the two of us. Gunter is somewhat relieved, since small talk isn't his specialty. I presume Hugo is never invited because he only eats rodents.

Varick pouts, however. Before now, he was teacher's pet. His kill rate earned him the honor.

He's still not back from wherever Eric sent him. I hope this is a good sign.

Still, I don't hold my breath. This meal marks the eighth day of this ordeal. My own one-hundred percent success rate has yet to win me what I want most: my husband's return.

Which is why I'm shocked when Eric declares, "If you finish all of your peaches in wine like a good girl, you can join me in my room for what you've been waiting for: seeing your husband alive and well."

Stunned, I sit up straight. "I'm ready to go now," I declare, pushing my dessert aside.

Eric shrugs, as if disappointed that the child in his care is so poorly mannered.

Sorry, but this is no time for politeness. I want to see Jack.

WHAT THE HELL? SERIOUSLY, I CAN'T BELIEVE WHAT I'M seeing!

In the video clip playing on the monitor in Eric's study, Jack lies on a bed while being massaged by a beautiful woman.

Massaged? That's putting it much too nicely. She's writhing all over him.

He seems to enjoy it. Why else is he smiling?

From the tenderness between them, I can tell this isn't the first time.

"Why, how dare he!" Emma's indignation comes in over my earbud loud and clear.

"Donna, that can't be Jack. It's got to be some kind of video sleight of hand," Ryan insists.

There is a newspaper on the dresser beside the bed. It shows yesterday's date.

All this time, I've worried over nothing?

Out of the corner of my eye, I catch Eric smothering his sly smile. It tells me what I need to know: *something is not right.*

Ryan commands, "Donna, time to get off this merry-go-round. Call his bluff." Noting my silence, he insists, "If he thinks he's lost you, he'll have to bring Jack home! Trust me on this."

Trust?

Trust is what I thought I had with Jack. Is what I just saw also a charade for the cameras, just one more thing he must do to stay alive?

Yes. It must be.

Otherwise, I'll kill him myself.

Time to prove Ryan right—I hope. "Thanks for this, Eric. It's all I need to know: Jack is alive and doing well." I walk toward the door.

"But…Mrs. Craig…perhaps you'd like to join me for a nightcap? I have your assignment for tomorrow—"

"I think not. It's been too long of a day. Frankly, it's been too long of a week. Too many assignments. I think I'll go home now."

He reaches the door before me. Blocking it, he says angrily, "So you're just going to leave him in my hands?"

I force out a chuckle. "Don't you mean in hers?"

Before he can respond I've shoved him out of the way and opened the door.

I've just stepped over the threshold when he says, "One more assignment. If you complete it successfully, he'll be waiting for you. If not, he dies."

His tone stops me cold. "I'll…think about it."

"Should you decide to take me up on the offer to save your husband's life, be ready by nine o'clock, sharp. Get a good night's sleep."

I nod and take my leave.

16

Jack's Diary, Day 8

Dear Donna,

Every day, I fight. Every day, I drive myself to win. Because if I fail, I die.

It's as simple as that.

And every day since I last saw you, I've presumed you've been doing your best to find me. Today, I found out just how far you'd go to save me.

Granted, it wasn't presented to me that way, but I have too much faith in you to think that you haven't considered the consequences of your actions.

I just hope you were wise enough to get Acme to cover your ass. Otherwise, should you be caught, it might all be for naught.

Let me start at the beginning:

By the time I got to the end of the tunnel leading into the plaza, or what was now known as *anillo de gladiadores*

—the gladiators' ring—two of my opponents were already there.

Both men had reasons to fight for their lives.

So did I, Donna. I needed to get back to you and the kids.

One of the men was a gringo: large, but soft, with bright red hair. The pale skin that goes with it was scorched bright red from the tropical sun. When he saw me, fear darkened his pale blue eyes. He mouthed my nickname: *El Santo.* A stream of piss trickled onto the dusty floor of his cage. The mob standing closest to him roared with laughter, some snickering at his shame with shouts of, "*¡No mames!*" and, "*¡A la verga!*"

"*Su nombre es* Dan Crawford," my guard, Jaime, grunted. "DEA." Noting my grimace, he added, "Not to worry, El Santo! Before he turned on El Maestro, he lied to your government. You do them both a favor."

My other opponent had at least six inches on me, and twice my size in girth. The moment he realized I'd entered the plaza, he stopped pacing his cage and cursing the crowd in order to glower at me. "Pedro Medina was the driver of El Maestro's chief rival, El Monstro," Jaime explained. "But he must pay the price for fucking his boss's favorite *puta.* If he lives, El Monstro will let him leave the country."

I wish I'd struck a similar deal with El Maestro. In any event, I wasn't planning on taking a fall because the dude couldn't keep his fly zipped.

When El Maestro finally appeared on the balcony, the

blonde stranger is still with him. Today, though, he is not smiling.

Neither is El Maestro.

The band stopped whatever it was playing in order to break into El Maestro's chosen theme song, "Besame mucho," which allowed him to serenade the crowd, as if the whole town were his own personal karaoke lounge.

If I didn't have to prep myself for possible death, I'd probably laugh.

El Maestro's gringo guest was just as amused, and snorted with laughter. Hearing it, El Maestro, furious, stopped mid-chorus. His head whipped around in the gringo's direction.

If anyone else had insulted one of Mexico's bloodiest drug lords, they would have stopped mid-chuckle, or at least faked a cough to cover up for this fatal faux pas. Not this dude. Instead, he had the audacity to slap El Maestro on the back, as if he was in on the sad joke about his inability to carry a tune.

El Maestro's eyes bulged in fury. Did the gringo realize what was happening? If he did, it didn't bother him because he just doubled up in laughter.

When El Maestro finally calmed down, he stared down into the plaza. His eyes landed on me. He snapped his fingers at Jaime.

Jaime released me into the plaza.

The crowd's frenzied roar caused Crawford to drop to his knees.

Its effect on Medina was less promising. Like a gorilla, he climbed the bars of his cage and shook his fist at me.

Since it was obvious Medina was going to be more of a challenge, El Maestro pointed to Crawford's cage first.

A guard came out with our weapons: a long chain, and a hatchet. As always, they were placed at opposite ends of the plaza.

And, as always, El Maestro took a handkerchief—but this time, it was not one from his wife, but snatched from the jacket of his gringo guest. He held it up for all to see before letting it fly off into a light breeze.

The second it hit the ground, Crawford was on the run—

Toward the axe.

Because I was savoring the look of hatred exchanged between my host and his guest, I moved a little slower. But that was okay. I realized that, for Crawford, the chain would do just as much damage.

BY THE TIME I HAD THE CHAIN WRAPPED AROUND MY FISTS, Crawford had grabbed the axe with both hands and was coming at me. Still, he waited until I stalked over to him to swing it, right to left like a batter going for the left-field bleachers.

I ducked just in time.

As I thought, the axe was heavy enough to pull him along for the ride, his arms still extended—

Giving me the opening I needed.

In order to get his footing, Crawford let go of the axe with his left hand. As the arm swung behind him, I caught his left wrist between both ends of the chain and jerked it toward me and down to the ground. He fell to his knees.

I pulled his open arm across my thigh and pressed down—so hard that his elbow, now braced against my leg, had nowhere to go.

As his forearm snapped, his howl echoed through the plaza.

There was enough chain left over for me to wrap it around his neck and gag his scream.

His bulging eyes stared up at me as he choked.

By the time he hit the ground he was a dead man.

Had Dan Crawford been a dirty cop? Did it matter?

He and I fought for our lives. I was the victor.

If it turned out Jaime was wrong, I'd have to live with the guilt.

FROM WHAT I COULD TELL, THE WHOLE TIME I WAS FIGHTING, Pedro Medina stood still, watching my every move.

He frowned when he saw how easy it was for me to take down Crawford.

He smiled when our weapons were tossed at our feet: karambit blades.

He picked up the short-handled knife. Palming it

under-handed, he then slashed the air with its small curved double-edged blade, as if practicing the moves he'd make on me.

When they opened his cage he charged me, snarling.

I crouched low, counting off his strides. When he was just a few feet away, I sprang upward.

My blade caught him in the gut, slicing a deep gash.

He shouted some obscenity, but was incensed enough to keep the knife in frenzied motion.

I was able to block or dodge most of his thrusts, but he got off a few slashes: one caught me on the shoulder, another in the back, and, when I kicked him away, below the knee.

The will to live is the greatest adrenaline rush. I know this first hand. But I also know the weariness that follows it, especially if the fight is long and arduous.

I didn't have the luxury of fatigue, Donna. I had to get back to you.

The fear that comes with it darkens the eyes and dulls the senses. The next thing you know, you're making stupid mistakes. In Pedro's case, it was a blocked lunge that put his face within stabbing reach of my karambit. As you know, Donna, the beauty of this little knife is that its blade ends in a curved point, like a tiger's tooth.

My jab caught his eyeball dead center.

Howling, he stumbled backward, only to trip over his own feet.

His knife flew out of his hand. He clawed the ground in the hope of finding it before I could get to him, but it was not to be. I landed hard, on his chest, with both knees, knocking the breath out of him.

My slash to his neck with the claw of the karambit went from his below his right ear to his left one. The blood squirting from both his jugular veins caught me square on my chest.

I was still wiping it off when the crowd's roar went off like a thunderclap.

I looked up at El Maestro for the last part of this dog-and-pony show: his tacit approval of my hollow victories, shown with a grudging nod before he waved good-bye to his minions. He was too preoccupied to savor my victory. It seemed that he was in a very heated discussion with the gringo. The next thing I knew, Blondie was being manhandled by a couple of El Maestro's thugs. They yanked him off his duff and out the door leading from the balcony.

At the time, I would have given anything to know what he'd said to get himself in Dutch with our host.

Little did I know that I'd soon find out.

NOW THAT MY OWN ROLE IN THIS SHOW OF STRENGTH WAS over, I walked toward the mouth of the cave buried deep within the bowels of El Maestro's palace, ignoring the cheers of a blood lusting mob that saw me as a savior, a saint, and an executioner. I knew there was no way to be all three.

"El Santo—no!" Jaime's hiss stopped me in my tracks.

I looked to where he pointed. El Maestro's thugs were goose-stepping Blondie into the plaza. When they reached the center, they tossed him to the ground.

He fell to his hands and knees.

A third guard strolled into the plaza. He carried three items. One, a pistol, was put on the north side of the plaza. The other things—a shield and long-handled axe, both of which looked to be from the medieval era—were left on the plaza's south side.

The crowd grew silent when they realized a third death match was about to take place.

As for me, well fuck it. I was tired of it all.

Granted, Blondie looked like a dandy, but we both know that looks can be deceiving.

I waited until he got up onto his feet. He took time to dust himself off, as if he were in no hurry. In hindsight, his casual stance was his way to assess the situation. Which weapon would best take me down? That was easy: the gun. But could he reach it in time? Maybe not. It depended on who had the greater will to live. Still, he realized it was worth the hustle in his bespoke John Lobbs.

El Maestro's explanation to the crowd was in Spanish. This was the gist of it: "Ladies and gentlemen, you're in for a treat!" He pointed toward Blondie. "My special guest, Varick Velesco, is an assassin in his own right, as world renowned as our own El Santo. Señor Velesco came as a friend to El Maestro. But as you all know, El Maestro's trust must be earned. In his case, it will not be easy." His very broad wink at the crowd drew a ripple of uncertain laughter. "It was Señor Velesco's wish to take El Santo from us. I am giving him the chance to do so. But something tells me that our El Santo will provide deliverance instead."

Is that what caused the rift between El Maestro and Velesco—his boast that he could take me down? I found it hard to believe.

El Maestro pointed at the gun. "The gladiators have been provided weapons from my own private collection: a six-shooter, and"—he shifted his arm to the other side of the plaza—"a shield, and an executioner's axe. The choice seems simple, yes? But no! You see, the gun holds only one bullet, whereas the axe's blade can deliver an infinite number of blows." El Maestro's smile morphed into a cruel grimace. "The choice is yours, Señor Velesco."

The crowd murmured its dismay at this change in policy.

Believe me, Donna, no one was more disappointed than me.

Varick Velesco took his time to weigh his choices. One bullet, and who knew in which chamber? In the meantime I could hack him to death.

Then again, considering his profession, if he released the shots in quick order, if he aimed right, I wouldn't live long enough to reach him.

I was not surprised when he nodded toward the gun.

From the broad smirk on El Maestro's face, neither was he.

It would have been interesting to know if El Maestro had promised Velesco his life in exchange for mine. My guess was yes. I was also willing to bet that he wouldn't honor it. In El Maestro's world, he was the only winner. If I went down, his sideshow went on with the hombre who took down El Santo.

To El Maestro's credit, he didn't drop the kerchief until Velesco and I had our weapons in hand.

The second the kerchief fell, Velesco took his first shot.

I ran straight at him with my shield raised so that it covered my head and torso. He could have moved, but he made the same choice I know I would have made: to stand his ground and pray that the bullet would be in the next cylinder of his barrel, and if so, that the shot would hit somewhere vital—my knee perhaps, or maybe my shin.

All the more reason I ran faster than I ever had in my life.

At the second click, I was only thirty feet away. I reached him after the fifth click, slamming him so hard that I lifted him off his feet—

And landed on top of him as he fell onto the plaza dirt floor.

He'd hit the back of his head. By the time I'd smacked

him in the face a few times with the shield, his nose was broken and gushing blood, and he'd swallowed a tooth. Still, he had the wherewithal to mutter, "You stupid fool! I was sent by Eric to get you out of here! But that Incan wannabe barbarian won't let you go. Not only are you his one-man goon squad, he's making suitcases full of money on your fights. And now he's coerced you to shoot the messenger—or in this case, chop off my head." He pointed to the axe—"You've got to keep me alive. Don't you get it? I'm your only ticket out of here!"

Was it possible that he was telling the truth? Was that what they'd quarreled about?

If his goal was to stop me in my tracks, he accomplished it.

But he lost all credibility when he took his last shot—point blank, at my face.

Donna, you should have seen the look on his face when he heard the sixth click and realized the last chamber was just as hollow as the other five.

It was as obvious to him as it was to me, El Maestro had set him up.

He threw the gun at me.

It cracked me on my cheek. Instinctively, I reeled back.

That gave him room to get on his feet. He grabbed the handle of the axe from the end, but I held onto it, high, on the neck. With all my might, using its blade as leverage, I tossed him onto the ground with me.

He hit his head when he fell, and it stunned him. I smiled, imagining his pain. Then I realized the agony was my own. While holding the blade, I'd sliced open my hand.

Despite being stunned from the fall, he was still lucid enough to mutter, "You're as stubborn as your cunt wife."

That earned him a few punches to his face. By the time I was done with him, his nose was a bloody pulp. "You know nothing of her," I growled.

"Sure I do." His chuckle was groggy, as if he were talking underwater instead of through broken teeth. "She's Quorum now."

"You're a liar!" I slammed the back of his head into the ground to make my point.

"Don't shoot the messenger, lover boy," he gasped. "It's her pact with the Devil—in this case, Eric Weber. She thought it would get you back. But now, with all she's done—documented, and ready to go to the enemies of her boyfriend, the President—she can't go back herself—and it's all because of you, lover boy."

Grief led me to let down my guard.

Varick tackled me at the knees. The axe flew out of my hand.

He scrambled for it, but I did too. Even if he were telling the truth, he was no use to me now.

Besides, I'd already killed too many to let him trick me to my death.

With lightning speed, he climbed to his feet, but I held fast to his left ankle, then bit his calf.

He howled as he once again fell to his knees. I rolled

out of reach, toward the axe. This time, when I had it, I had no doubt what I had to do: put him out of his misery.

A single quick swing severed his head from his neck.

The mob gasped as Varick's head rolled toward *El Maestro's* balcony. It stopped face-up.

Varick's glassy eyes stared up at me.

I picked up his head by its golden curls, and held it up to *El Maestro.*

The crowd roared its approval.

I wanted to throw up. Instead, I tossed Varick's head at him.

His initial instinct was to duck, but then he manned up and caught it. When he did, he let loose with a half-hearted chortle.

The mob went into a frenzy. To the crowd's collective mind, the gladiators were a live video game playing out in front of their eyes in 3D. Should the splatter of blood reach a bystander or two, they'd stare at it silently for a moment before breaking into laughter with the rest of the mob.

The best part of the death matches was the euphoria of being the one left standing. I'd laugh too—

Until I remembered I'd have to do this yet again, tomorrow.

As I left the field of battle, their cheers were still ringing in my ears.

17

Fantasies

Wives, there are a few incidences when it's okay for you to fantasize about someone who isn't your husband. Specifically, they are:

1. *When the man in question is a previous crush, but you've never acted on your desire for him. Lady, you are a saint!*
2. *When the man in question is a celebrity, because let's face it: the odds that he'll leave his celebrity wife for you are slim to none.*
3. *When the length of your husband's absence borders on the possibility that he can be declared legally dead. Time to give up the ghost.*

Gentlemen, there are no circumstances in which you may fantasize about other women. That is all.

I am dreaming of Jack.

It is I who massage him, not her.

His naughty grin is for me, not her.

He lifts the hem of my white gauzy skirt over my hips in order to enter me, not her.

He never made love to her at all. I know that.

I only love you, Donna.

The sound of his voice in my mind is so clear and so true that I bolt straight up in bed. When I open my eyes, I know I'll see him, standing before me.

But no, it's not Jack in front of me.

Eric sits in the chair beside my bed.

I glance at the clock. It's three in the morning. How long has he been watching me?

"It's time that I told you about your next assignment." There is no longer any playfulness in his voice.

"I'm…ready." I hesitate because I realize I'm not wearing my earbuds or surveillance lenses. No one at Acme is monitoring this conversation.

"It's big of you to forgive me for your husband's… indiscretion." He places a photo face down on the bed beside me. "Your final assignment is an extermination. You're to be accompanied only by Gunter, so that he can confirm the kill. Having presumed your remorse over 'killing the messenger'—figuratively if not literally— Varick is already in transit to oversee your husband's safe passage home. That being said, the sooner the extermination takes place, the sooner you will be reunited with your husband."

He walks out the door.

THE TARGET IS RYAN.

I drop down slowly onto the bed, stunned.

I've got to let him know, so that we can work this out…

There is a knock on the door.

It's Gunter. He holds an attaché case.

Before I can stop him, he pushes his way in. "Let's go."

"I've got to pack up—"

"Done."

He's right. I look around the room. Except for black slacks and a matching jacket, all of my things are gone, including my valise and purse.

My surveillance lenses and earbuds are hidden in the heels of my boots.

"But—but I have to make contact the right way with… the target."

"Mr. Weber has already taken care of it." His grin is cruel. "Mr. Clancy has been told that we are holding you hostage. You are to be released in exchange for some intelligence that we know he possesses."

"He would never agree to it! He values the security of our country above all else, even the lives of his operatives—"

It's the opposite of everything Ryan stands for, but I'll be damned if I let him know it.

"Foolish bitch! Don't you think we already know this? But, yes, he has agreed to do so, and is preparing false intelligence so that he can save you and his reputation at the same time. While he's waiting for you on a park bench, you'll be spotting him through this."

He opens the attaché. It holds a Remington 700 sniper rifle.

He closes it again, and nods toward the door. "We've got a bit of a drive ahead of us, so you'd better get a move on. You've got only five minutes to dress."

I take four of those minutes to pray.

I'm out the door in five and a half minutes.

IT TAKES US ALMOST THREE HOURS TO GET TO OUR destination: the Red Rock Canyon Trail, high in the ochre-hued hills that make up Trabuco Canyon's Whiting Ranch Wilderness Park.

Already, Gunter's cigarette smoke is getting to me. By the time Ryan gets here, he will have gone through his whole pack of cigs.

Those things will be the death of him—hopefully, sooner than later.

Eric has thought of everything. The bench sits deep into the trail and around the bend of the trail with a distractingly straight-on view of the ocean, the ledge I will shoot from gives me coverage and the perfect straight-on kill shot, once Ryan takes a seat.

When the bullet hits, he'll be admiring a spectacular sunrise over the canyon's deep copper-hued hills.

I know he'll be thinking of Natalie.

"HE'S HERE." GUNTER LOWERS HIS CIGARETTE IN ORDER TO point at the bear-like figure lumbering up the trail. I'd recognize it anywhere.

Ryan wears workout pants, a pullover running jacket, sunglasses, and a baseball cap on his balding head. He stops directly in front of the bench, looks around, and then flops down onto it as he heaves a labored sigh.

He stares out at the view for a moment, then checks his watch. When he's done, he pulls a water bottle from his jacket pocket and guzzles from it.

Ryan is here for only one reason: he thinks he's saving my life.

My children have already lost one father, maybe two. He wants to make sure that they don't lose yet another parent.

That night at his cabin—my God, it seems so long ago! —he told me himself that, if he had it to do all over again, he would have put Natalie and their unborn child before job and country.

And now it's my turn.

He is my chance to save my family. To save Jack.

Oh, Ryan, I wish it didn't have to be this way.

I wait until his eyes look back at the vista before lining him up in my sight, and aiming for his chest.

Gently, I pull the trigger.

The suppressor muffles the sound, but the vapor trail proves that my nightmare is now reality.

When the bullet pierces his chest, he slams into the back of the bench.

Blood darkens the entry wound. His head slumps to one side. If anyone were to wander by, they'd think he'd fallen asleep.

I lean back, stunned at my action. Only then do I notice Gunter has his cellphone pointed at me.

"Smile and say cheese," he taunts, smirking.

Fury heats up my face. I swing the gun around directly into his face—

But I know better than to pull the trigger.

When Gunter finally realizes he won't be joining Ryan as vulture food, he stumbles angrily down the hillside toward the bench. When he reaches it, he takes Ryan's pulse, both at his wrist and his neck.

He nods up at me, and then signals me to follow him down the trail, the way we arrived.

Forgive me, Ryan.

Forgive me, God.

~

WE DRIVE AWAY IN SILENCE.

I'm still so upset about Ryan that I don't even notice where Gunter is taking me until, a half-hour later, he pulls up to the front of my honeymoon hotel in Laguna Beach.

I tap him on the shoulder. "Why are we here?"

"You want to be waiting at the right place for your husband, don't you?"

I lean back. I still can't believe I'll soon hold Jack in my arms.

I still can't believe I killed Ryan.

Gunter unlocks my door, but he doesn't get out.

"Aren't you coming in?" I ask.

"Wait in your room until Mr. Weber calls."

He roars off.

I head to the elevator. The boy at the front desk barely looks up from his cellphone's screen.

Just like old times.

I WAIT UNTIL MIDNIGHT, BUT ERIC NEVER CALLS.

I doze off by two.

At six in the morning, there is a knock on the door. I rouse myself, then stumble to answer it. Jack—

But, no. It's the kid from the front desk. "This is for you." He holds a large giftwrapped box in his hands.

When I take it, he warns me, "Heavier than it looks, so don't drop it."

I wait until he's caught the elevator before I take it into my room and shut the door.

THE BOX IS TWO FEET SQUARE, ON ALL SIDES. A LARGE WHITE bow is taped to its top.

An iPhone is tied to the center of the bow.

Warily, I open the box top—

A head is inside.

I close the top and sit down.

I lift the top once more and force myself to look inside:

It's Varick.

One of his eyelids is closed. He looks as if he's winking about some secret we share.

When I can no longer stand it, I close the box top again. All I can think of is, Thank God it isn't Jack.

I pick up the phone. One click puts it on default mode, to video.

What I see stuns me: Jack, dirty, sweaty, bruised, and carrying a long-handled axe and a shield, stands in some sort of plaza encircled by a cheering crowd.

Suddenly, he runs directly at Varick, who is firing a gun at him.

By the time Jack is face to face with him, Varick realizes the pistol had no bullets. He throws the gun. It hits Jack's face.

Varick tries to wrestle the axe away, but Jack is too strong for him.

Varick, with that sly smirk of his, says something to Jack that stuns him enough to let his guard down, if only for a moment. It's just long enough for Varick to make his move for Jack's axe. He trips Jack and scoops it up, but Jack grabs ahold of his leg and takes a bite. The pain causes Varick to drop it.

Jack grabs it, and swings.

Varick's head rolls as it hits the ground.

Jack picks it up and holds it high, in victory.

The video ends in a freeze frame.

Jack…killed Varick?

Is this to be Jack's fate—to fight to the death?

Where the hell is he? Is he now dead too?

Jack will never come back to me.

It's taken me only ten days to become a widow once more.

I run to the toilet and throw up.

When I can finally collect myself, I head toward the door with the phone. No, I'm not taking Eric's present too. I mean, what if a cop pulls me over?

And I certainly can't call Acme and ask that they send a cleaner—

Not after what I've just done to Ryan.

I stop, though, to move the DO NOT DISTURB sign to the outside of the doorknob. This hotel has already lost one maid. The way this place is run, I can't imagine they can afford to lose any more.

By nine, I am home.

I swing onto Hilldale Avenue, which goes right down

the center of town. The street is bustling with shoppers who carry bags of all sizes with logos from its many posh shops. I should recognize the faces, but my mind only sees one wherever I look:

Ryan's.

On an early summer morning, everyone is puttering around their well-kept yards. Wives are trimming rose bushes and husbands are mowing lawns. The sidewalks and yards are filled with children who giggle as they play.

This is what normal looks like.

Mothers with prams head for Hilldale Memorial Park. I must drive by it before reaching my home. There is a game in play on the baseball diamond. What time is it? Only nine o'clock? Jeff's game is at four o'clock. I'll be able to make it—

But not Jack.

I'm back to square one: I have to find my husband.

How do I tell my children that he may never come home to us?

"Mom!" Mary yells from her bedroom window as I pull into the driveway. Evan's head pops out of it too. Noting my frown, he waves at me weakly, but then ducks inside again.

A moment later, though, both are hurtling down the stairs and out the door. Jeff and Trisha are on their heels. Aunt Phyllis is not far behind.

It's a group hug. Everyone is talking at once—

Everyone but me.

It takes a while for them to notice this. When they do, they ask in unison: "Where's Dad?"

Smile. Keep smiling. Just…smile.

The lie comes out all too easily: "He's needed in the office, so I dropped him off there first."

Trisha collapses in my arms with a scowl, whereas Mary and the boys express their disappointment with groans. "Will he still make my game?" Jeff asks anxiously.

"Yes, of course." This is a very, very bad dream.

Assured, they nod and make their way back into the house. Evan is gentlemanly enough to take my valise in with him.

I take my time meandering through the yard. One might think I'm admiring the riot of color that greets me in my rose garden, but in truth, I have a purpose. I need to get somewhere that gives me privacy, and quick:

The playhouse.

The old wrought iron daybed squeaks as I lay on it. The faces of Mary and Trisha's old dolls stare out at me from every nook and corner. Their blank eyes are filled with accusation and disgust.

I had to do it—for Jack.

I duck under the bed's careworn quilt, as if I can hide from the truth of my actions over the past ten days:

I killed Ryan.

Jack is dead.

Eric lied all along.

18

Jack's Diary, Day 9

"EL MAESTRO WISHES THAT YOU JOIN HIM FOR THIS EVENING, in celebration of your victories." Lola's murmur roused me from my dream of us.

That is to say, you and me, my darling Donna. In it, we were wrapped in each other's arms on some warm beach. The tide swept in and around us, cooling our skin, if not the passion we share for each other.

From now on, I'll associate vanilla and almond essences with you, sweet wife.

I open one eye. Lola is blushing, as if she'd read my thoughts. Her mysticism showed itself in numerous ways.

I'm glad I'm lying on my stomach. Otherwise, Lola might misconstrue the reason for my erection. Granted, it doesn't help that, for the past hour she has been massaging my tired muscles with her magic potions. Killing three men yesterday—Blondie and the two before him—has taken its toll on me. El Maestro has finally acknowledged that I'm only human and has given me the day off. Even thoroughbred horses are given a rest between races.

"What do you suspect El Maestro wants?" I asked.

"He wishes to celebrate your wins with you. There will be *un paseo público*—a public procession—in your honor, with music, costumes, and fireworks. You will watch it with him from his private balcony."

"Costumes?" I can't help but smirk. "Like, 'Day of the Dead?'"

"*Sí, Dia de Muertos.* The revelers will either dress as you, or in memory of those you've killed." A tear rolled down her cheek. She was thinking of my first kill: Miguel. "It is at El Maestro's behest that the women dress in white, like virgins."

When I reach out for her, she sidesteps my hand.

"Maybe I'll pass on the honor." But of course, I'll be there. I'll do anything to escape this cage. The dinner will be my chance to leave, one way or another.

She freezes, but only for a moment. After all, we're still on El Maestro's *Candid Camera.* I feel her toes dig into my thighs as she rises over me. She squeezes hard on my shoulders as she massages them. Then, softly: "You promised." Her declaration is softer than the breeze that is filtering through the high barred window.

Fulfilling my promise may get us both killed.

Still, I couldn't leave her in this hellhole. What he

would do to her is unthinkable. We both know it. "Yes, and I meant what I said."

Her hands move down my spine: prodding, pressing, caressing, as if thanking me.

Perhaps warning me.

As her fingers roll over my calves, she murmurs, "I leave you a present: a new potion. *Es veneno.* A drop on his fork or in his drink and he is *muerto.*"

Ah, a poison.

Now she moves up my back. Rolling her knuckles across my shoulders she mutters, "The mirror on the wall of his office wall leads into a secret tunnel. Go west."

"How do you know this?"

"Miguel found the architectural drawings in city hall. He dreamt of a coup."

I dream of escape. I say a prayer of thanks in his name.

Our little show goes on for another fifteen minutes. Finally, Lola's supple, knowing hands fall away from my body. She rises off me with a sigh. I pretend to sleep as she taps the bars on the door with her nails, alerting the guard that she is ready to leave.

His footsteps echo on the concrete floor as he makes his way over. The key clinks as it enters the lock.

"*¡Mira aquí!* El Maestro wishes that El Santo wears this tonight. I'll be back in an hour, to escort him." Through the cracked mirror against the wall, I watch as Jaime hands Lola a suit. It is black, as is the shirt beneath it. No tie.

Very gangster. And perfect for my escape.

Lola takes it and hangs it over one of the straight back chairs.

The door clinks shut again. Her footsteps follow his down the hall.

I wait another ten minutes before getting up from my bench and going over to the suit. Yes, it is my size.

I dress with care, since there is always the chance that I might die in this suit, but I think not. Kill in it, yes. And, I'll do so in style.

I head back over to the bench, where I notice a tiny vial beside a folded towel.

The poison will buy me time to find Lola, perhaps.

In any event, I will escape.

Forgive me, Lola, if I don't do both.

THERE IS NO ODDER FEELING THAN SEEING YOUR FACE covering the faces of hundreds of others, all of whom are marching toward you to the beat of mariachi music.

Every now and again, the bands stop in front of El Maestro's balcony in order to serenade us. There are other masks as well—some of El Maestro—but not many of them.

The procession, almost an hour long, is nearing its end. On the hill flanking the other side of the plaza, the small army of men who have set up the fireworks display await El Maestro's signal to light up the dark sky.

On the breath of the night wind, tumbleweeds roll

from one side to the other, kicking up skirts of dust from the dry ground. They gild the bodies of my victims, which, at my host's orders, were tied to high posts throughout the plaza, as a deterrent to any intentions to defy him.

As Lola pointed out, it led to the assumption that I serve El Maestro as his executioner.

Yes, I am. He's about to find out.

"You see, *gringo*—they love you!" El Maestro shouts above the loud din, then slaps me on the back. "Look at how many virgins smile at you! If I command it, they will gladly give themselves to you." He chuckles. "Perhaps, *Santo*, we will take them together, eh?"

I shake my head. "Not interested. I hold to my vows."

El Maestro laughs heartily. His eyes shift to Lola, who had the task of serving us our food and drink. I eat very little of it. Watching El Maestro drool over Lola is enough to make anyone lose his appetite.

Throughout the meal, he patted and groped her whenever she was within reach. All the more reason she ended every course beside the ornate antique sideboard that is laden with all sorts of delicacies: trout in a black bean sauce, *pollo molè, arroz con pollo,* and a mélange of stewed and grilled vegetables. The meal is served with award-winning California wines. This monster is no stranger to the good life.

Noting her slight blush and the look of longing in her eyes when I glance her way, his smile collapses into a grimace.

What he doesn't know is that she isn't mourning for my unrequited love, but for that of her fallen Miguel's. For his executioner, she has already granted absolution.

For his mortal enemy, El Maestro, she plans his murder.

Did I bring Lola's vial of poison? No. I knew I'd never slip it by the guards who frisked me before I entered El Maestro's private quarters.

But from the looks of things, I won't need it.

A far wall is covered with El Maestro's prized possessions: his antique weapons collection. I'm personally familiar with several of them.

Hello, old friends. Glad to have you so close by.

El Maestro walks over to the balcony. He gives the high sign to the men on the hill to prepare to start the fireworks.

Any moment now…

Lola puts a small round platter on the table: apples, pears, and mangos are nestled among wedges of various hard cheeses. One of the wedges is pierced with a small paring knife.

Our host clicks his tongue at Lola to get her attention. When her eyes finally meet his, he nods toward the vast liquor bar at the other end of the room, where a bottle of very expensive port sits on a silver tray with two glasses.

She purses her lips. Her eyes dart from side to side. Slowly, she steels herself to walk over to it and pick it up.

She's poisoned his port.

"Que linda, la virgen, eh?" El Maestro pats Lola's

bottom as she pours the port into one of the glasses and puts it in front of him.

I shrug. "*Si, que linda.*"

El Maestro pulls her into his lap and nuzzles her neck.

With all her might, she slaps his face.

He stands up, roaring. With an elbow to her back, he shoves her down onto the table with one hand, while unzipping his pants with the other. Bending over her, he hisses, "No more disrespect, *puta*! El Santo may not want you, but I do. Not to worry. He'll enjoy watching your deflowering. All men do. Stop your struggling, *puta*. Who knows? It might fan the fire of lust you'd hoped he'd have for you."

At the same time he kicks her legs apart, he slaps her head on the table so hard that she whimpers, but she has quit struggling. She lays there, shivering and mouthing prayers as he positions himself between her legs.

The thrust is deep, and draws a whimper from her as he leans into her and gasps a curse into her ear.

But Lola isn't the one who has been penetrated. The paring knife, sharp and shiny, went between his ribs and pierced a kidney just as smoothly as if it were butter.

It comes out just as easily. As he quivers through his death throes, I wonder if I should grant him the courtesy he never gave his oppressors: that of a quick death?

I think of the priest and of Miguel as I jerk back his head with one hand and run the knife against his throat with the other.

Just as he collapses on top of Lola, the fireworks begin.

The sky lights up as if a war has started.

It hasn't yet. The spoils of his diabolical kingdom will go to the victor among the *narcos*, who will soon begin another bloody war with one another.

Lola and I won't be around to see it.

I shove El Maestro's body to one side. She shakes as she clutches my hand, and stumbles with me to the vast mirror on the wall. We twist the sconce that moves the mirror to one side. The staircase it hides falls so steeply that it might as well be taking us into Hell.

I remind myself that this is only an illusion. In truth, these are the steps that will take me to you.

I push the lever that closes the mirror once more, and we begin our descent.

THERE IS A LIGHT AT THE END OF THE STAIRCASE. FOR THE past five minutes, we've been following its glow to our final destination.

Lola was right that the stairs end in a hall that leads in two directions. The one that goes east is the shortest— twenty feet at most. It must open into a basement corridor.

I head in that direction.

"El Santo, that is the wrong way!" Lola tugs at my sleeve.

"I know. But I've got some unfinished business. You

go on ahead. Leave Paraíso now, Lola—before they come looking for you."

She nods, then shakes her head. "I stay with you."

Her nobility astounds me.

Still, she just made my mission a little harder. I now have two reasons to stay alive.

As I thought, the door opens next to El Maestro's meth lab. How had One-Eyed Juan put it? Oh yeah. El Maestro was an artist. Meth was his medium.

Well, you know what they say: art is subjective.

The hall window's curtains are open. No one is in the lab. They are all outside, watching the fireworks.

The real ones are just about to begin.

The room is filled with at least twenty vats. I move from one to another, raising the temperatures to as far up as they will go.

Seeing me, Lola follows my lead.

We get all but eight of them when someone walks by the half-glass wall—a guard. He glances in.

I hiss to Lola, "Get down!"

Too late, the guard sees her.

She turns around to find him staring at her.

He draws his AK-47 and rushes through the door.

I roll behind it.

The heavy metal door bursts open. He points his gun at her. "*¿Quién eres? ¿Por qué estás aquí?*"

To answer his question as to who she is, she raises her hands and smiles. "They want me to clean up in here."

I slam the door into the man.

Instinctively, he pulls the trigger.

A bullet from his AK-47 hits Lola. She hits the floor like a rag doll.

Other bullets hit the tanks around her.

I leap out from behind the door, onto the floor, and slide as far down the hall as possible.

The impact throws the guard through the glass and into the hallway.

Even a five-hundred year-old stone palace can't stand a blast of this magnitude. The explosion goes up and out. I barely make it into the tunnel, shutting the door behind me.

Then I run like hell.

THE TUNNEL MUST RUN FOR TWO MILES UNDERGROUND. IT ends at a staircase that climbs up some thirty feet. I wonder what will be waiting for me there.

Hopefully, not a platoon of armed guards.

When I get to the door at the top, I look through the peephole at the darkness beyond.

I hear nothing.

I open the door, just a crack. Then wider.

That's when I see him: Abu.

"What the—"

He grabs me in a bear hug. He's not the only one. George Taylor, one of Acme's pilots, is also there.

And so is Jaime. He grins as he flips open his badge. "Undercover DEA," he explains. "Your boss put out feelers about any gringos in the custody of El Maestro. At the same time, your men here"—he nods toward Abu and George—"flew Varick Velesco here from Los Angeles. That confirmed it."

"How did you know my getaway would lead me here?"

"Lola. She and Miguel have been quite helpful to us." His smile fades. "I presume the fact that she isn't here with you is a bad sign."

I nod. "She helped me blow up El Maestro's meth lab and got shot for her efforts." I frown at the thought. "What did Velesco say to get him on El Maestro's bad side?"

"That he was taking El Maestro's *verdugo* home with him. El Maestro didn't like that. So he gave Velesco a choice: if he beat you, he'd be allowed to live. He realized that either way, he wouldn't be bringing you home." Jaime shrugs. "You were quite a little cash cow for El Maestro, something for him to throw in the faces of the other *narcos*. Sadly, Jack, you may have started a trend with these gladiator events. In the meantime, El Maestro's territory is up for grabs, so I have my work cut out for me."

Abu pats me on the shoulder. "Let's get going before they discover we're here."

I hop into Jaime's truck with Abu and George. As we roar off down the road, I ask, "Donna isn't here?"

The looks exchanged between George and Abu tell me all I need to know:

Something is terribly wrong.

ABU INSISTS ON TELLING ME ONLY AFTER WE'RE WHEELS UP:

That you, Donna, became a double agent for the Quorum, in order to win my release;

That sometime within the past six hours, Ryan has been killed;

And that according to the NSA, you, my dear wife, were his executioner.

I shake my head adamantly. "I don't fucking believe you! Where did you hear that bullshit?"

"Look, Jack, don't shoot the messengers." Abu throws up his hands. "I'm just relaying intel that is coming from Acme headquarters. Because we're down here, we've been out of the loop!"

"How would the NSA know about Ryan's death before Acme?"

"Because of previous kidnapping attempts, apparently all Covert Ops directors and their loved ones must wear subcutaneous tracking chips. Ryan resisted doing so—until recently. I think your kidnapping convinced him to comply."

"Makes sense," I admit.

"As it turns out, when Donna came to him about your plight and her dilemma—accepting Eric Weber's tasks in exchange for your release—Ryan injected her with a tracking chip too—so that we wouldn't lose sight of her while she was undercover with the Quorum. But as part of the deal, Donna insisted that only your mission team could know of your kidnapping."

I nod. "I would have done the same."

"We've had video and audio contact with her the whole time—up until last night. Then she went dark. In the meantime, Ryan was killed, and Donna's tracker put her at the scene of his murder."

"It still doesn't mean that she pulled the trigger."

"No, it doesn't. But it validates an anonymous video link the NSA received just an hour ago. It shows her taking the kill shot." Abu frowns. "In the meantime, Eric and his bodyguards, Gunter and Hugo, have disappeared." He shrugs. "Dominic, Emma, and Arnie are being briefed by POTUS. We're to land at Lion's Lair so that we can join them. By then, I'm sure Donna will be picked up as well."

He doesn't say the obvious: *unless she left with Eric.*

And then I remember Varick's taunts.

Donna, what the hell have you done?

19

Be Polite to Your Partner

Wives, the easiest way to show your love and respect to your husbands is to be polite. Use this rule of thumb: treat him as you hope he'd treat you. For example:

1. *Never be rude to his parents. By setting a good example, perhaps he'll follow it too.*
2. *Never walk into the bathroom when he's sitting on the throne. It's not the best look on a man. And despite your protestations otherwise, there are a few situations where it's hard to look ladylike. This one ranks high on the list for you too.*
3. *Never come home drunk out of your gourd. That way, you lead by example that he should not either.*
4. *And, finally, don't borrow his lipstick. For that matter, the fact that he wears any should make you wonder where his mouth has been.*

"Mom! Mom!" Mary's voice sounds frantic. "There are some men here to see you. They're from…from Lion's Lair!"

Lion's Lair.

Lee.

I rise slowly from the day bed to meet my fate.

My husband may be dead. My boss is, for sure.

I don't know how long I've sat in the playhouse. All I know is that the late afternoon sun is no longer overhead, but that the dappled light coming in through the window is at a slant.

Before I open the door, I do my best to alter the look on my face from guilt to curiosity. I can't let Mary read the truth within it. Not yet, anyway. I need time to grieve.

Mary holds my hand as I walk through the yard. The men are waiting at my back door. They flash badges embossed with the NSA logo.

I assure them that I'm Donna Stone Craig.

When they ask me to accompany them to Lion's Lair, Mary clasps my hand so tightly that I think she'll break a finger.

"It's okay," I assure her. "I'll be home soon."

"Will Dad be home soon too?" she asks softly.

I think of the many times she asked that very question of me in the five years during Carl's disappearance. My heart broke each time then. It does so now, too, because I can't answer her.

Realizing this, tears fill her eyes.

As I'm driven away, I don't look back.

I AM ESCORTED OUTSIDE LEE'S OFFICE, AND TOLD TO TAKE A seat on the sofa opposite Eileen's desk.

If she's a ghost hovering anywhere about, I'm sure she's laughing at my dilemma.

The heavy, brisk steps coming from the hallway stop when they reach Eileen's door. They warn me that several men are about to join me.

My firing squad?

No. It is Jack. At his side are Abu and George.

I run to my husband and shower him with kisses—

So, why isn't he kissing me back?

He stands there with his hands by his side. He looks everywhere but at my face.

I don't understand. After all I've done—for him? Indignantly, I ask, "Jack! What's wrong?"

His lids fall heavily. When he opens them again, it is to stare at me with cold sad eyes. Finally, he mutters, "Ryan."

I try to wipe my tears before he sees them, but they fall too fast.

"Donna…" His voice chokes with despair. "How could you?"

How could I?

I could—and I *did*—

For him.

I turn away. The accusation hurts more than if he had backhanded me across the cheek.

I'm just about to scream that at him when Lee's door opens.

Ryan stands there.

Jack and I stare at him, then each other.

Ryan beckons to us. "You two kids have had quite a honeymoon. Come on in."

Jack and I rise in unison.

But when he tries to take my hand, I jerk it away, and walk in.

"HOW DID YOU KNOW?" I LOOK DIRECTLY AT RYAN.

"Your tracker led us to the Montage. We booked the rooms below Eric's so that Arnie could set up additional surveillance."

But of course.

"When Eric gave you the assignment of killing me, we were concerned you'd balk," Ryan continues. "To tell you the truth, I was somewhat surprised with how easily you accepted it."

"Oh! …Well…you know, I was trying to stall…buying time…"

Ryan's laugh is the loudest in the room.

Jack isn't laughing at all.

Neither am I.

Finally, I mutter, "I know the rifle had real bullets. So, how did you fake your death, Ryan?"

"I was wearing the latest and greatest concealable body armor." Ryan smiles supremely.

"But…there was blood—"

"It was a squib. You know, fake blood, like they do in the movies," Arnie explains. "Since Ryan was going to be hit by some projectile, we didn't need to detonate remotely. Usually, we'd use a Bobcat—"

"He means a tiny rocket fuse," Emma butts in. "The blood—we used the real stuff, not the non-smell fake stuff, since we were concerned about Gunter's verification —was packed into condoms that filled the whole inside of Ryan's windbreaker. She sighs. "I guess it's one way to get rid of some of that ten-year supply we've got in our laundry room—"

"Not for lack of trying," Arnie gives Lee a thumbs-up.

I'm so happy to see that Lee ignores him. Time to change the subject. "Ryan, how did you slow your pulse?"

"Right before I walked into sight, I stuck myself with an Epipen containing an extreme sedative that slowed my heartbeat to barely alive. We had to wait until I recovered to bring you in on it. Otherwise, the NSA would have had a right to charge you with terrorism." His gaze slides to Lee.

Lee smiles at me. "They're not Donna's greatest fans, but I'm working on it."

Jack's scowl grows larger.

Lee ignores it. "As it turns out, Jack got here just in time to get in on these secrets. Jack, while you were in transit, DEA agent Jaime Mendoza filled us in on your tribulations under El Maestro. You conducted yourself brilliantly. You'll be rewarded with a Prisoner of War medal."

"Thanks. Yeah, dealing with *narcos*—just follow their lead and play by the book." His sarcasm puts a frown on everyone's face, including mine.

"The woman giving you a rubdown wasn't in any book I know of," I mutter, "Unless it was written by Sylvia Day."

Jack's head whips in my direction. "No need to be jealous—even if she hadn't been killed while helping me escape."

I can't say anything to that. So instead, bite my lip to keep from crying out, *why do you care so much? What about my sacrifice?*

Lee winces, but being the ultimate diplomat, he turns to Jack. "I know you went through hell. I want to thank you for your service to your country."

"Don't thank me," Jack says evenly. "Do us all a favor and take real action against the *narcos*. They're the ones breaking up our families—not to mention those in our neighboring country. And by action, I don't mean by legalizing even more drugs, like meth and heroin. As long as killers like El Maestro are making billions of dollars with exports of drugs to our country, they'll continue to pay off politicians—on both sides of the border—and this reign of terror is going to continue. Time to follow the money."

"I'll put it on my to-do list." Lee's tone is as cold as ice.

Before Jack can retort, Ryan turns to Emma. "Why don't you fill the team in on the contents of Eileen's blue envelope?"

Emma nods. "Each line held a different encryption. The first was the location of the digital cloud containing audio and video files of the president's Oval Office and Lion's Lair meetings."

"We were able to scrub those before Eric could access them," Arnie adds. "To explain the empty file, we also left a note that can only be traced back to Eileen. It requests more money for providing the files. I'm sure Eric's head exploded when he read it. Now that she's dead, he'll never really know what happened to them."

"The other encryption contained a list of Quorum investments, along with its three Swiss bank accounts," Emma continues. "We've left the money intact. However, we embedded a Trojan into the accounts. That way, whenever Eric transfers money out, we can follow the trail."

"It's time to take Eric down." Jack's declaration doesn't leave room for argument.

"Agreed. And I think you're the man—and Donna is the woman—to do it." Ryan takes each of our hands in his before putting them together. "Donna, you know me well enough that I would never disagree with the decision that you made to follow through on Eric's order. You did the right thing—for Jack, and for your family." He looks me in the eye. "Since the moment Eric Weber came into your lives—separately, and jointly—he's done his best to ruin them. But he hasn't succeeded because you love each other. Because, together, you are a family."

Is Jack still of part of our family?

Does he still love me?

I guess I'll soon find out.

EMMA LENDS US HER CAR SO THAT JACK AND I HAVE A RIDE home from Lion's Lair. "Sorry about the stinky diaper in the backseat." She wrinkles her nose. "Nicky always goes boom-boom at the worst times! I didn't want to carry it into Lion's Lair with me."

Finally, I've got something to laugh at. "I don't blame you. Where is the little guy now?"

"Arnie's retrieving him from Janie's wing. Lee insisted that her au pair could watch him." Emma laughs. "I'm just glad it's not Frannie. Now, that would have been scary!"

She tosses the keys to me, but Jack snatches them first.

"I'll drive," he growls.

I shrug. "Then I'll walk home."

Emma sighs. "I'm out of here." She disappears back inside Lion's Lair.

Jack gets into the car and starts the engine.

I start down the hill.

He passes me with a wave.

He gets a middle-finger salute in return.

Still, he's waiting for me just beyond the guardhouse at the beginning of the estate's private lane. As I walk by, he rolls down the window. "Get in. I don't want the neighbors gossiping about you again."

"Since when do you care what they say?"

"Since you became my wife."

"I can remedy that for you easily with a quickie divorce. No need to go to Mexico for it either. I'll just take the next flight to Las Vegas—"

He's out of the car.

He's got me in his arms.

He's kissing me.

I'm kissing back.

He rests his arms on my shoulders so that we're eye-to-eye and heart to heart. "Donna Craig, I'd follow you to the ends of the Earth to stay at your side."

"Since when? Since it dawned on you that the only reason I chose to sacrifice Ryan was in order to save you?"

"You're right. It was hard for me to hear you agreed to murder our boss. At the same time, I can't blame you. It's exactly the choice I would have made if it would have brought you home to me." The thought sobers him. "Apparently, Ryan feels the same way."

I lean into his kiss.

When our lips part, I warn him, "We still need to talk —about...everything. Not now, but soon."

Jack nods. "Agreed." He knows I mean Lola. And I'm sure he's got some questions of his own. An idea puts a smile on his face. "Want to go back to our honeymoon suite? We've still got one more day on our reservation."

Now it's my turn to laugh. When I tell him about Varick's head, he gets it: three's a crowd.

"That's okay," he replies. "Like you said, we'll talk later. Right now, I'm dying to see the kids."

Works for me.

We only drive half a block when I begin gagging from the stinking diaper. "Phew! I realize now that I'm not the only reason you got out of the car!"

The way in which he shrugs shows me I'm right.

Can we hold our breath until we pull into the driveway? One way or another we'll pass out, so it's worth the gamble.

JOY IS THE LOOK IN YOUR CHILDREN'S EYES WHEN YOU WALK in and say, "We're home!"

Happiness comes with the crush of their hugs, the dampness of their kisses, and the vows they request that you'll never go away for so long again.

Love is the knowledge that they don't want to live without you.

When Jeff asks us what we did on our honeymoon other than "all that yucky stuff," Jack entwines his fingers in mine before answering. "Nothing else. Everything we did was yucky, horrible, terrible—" He grins knowingly at Jeff. "You get the picture."

It's not a lie. I'm glad, because I always want to keep our promise to tell our children the truth.

Jeff must be picturing something because his face turns bright red. Aunt Phyllis is too, because she snorts, while Trisha giggles.

Mary smiles through her tears. Evan puts his arm around her for a quick squeeze.

Suddenly, I'm glad she has someone to confide in.

Jeff pumps his fist into the air. "Since you're home, you can come to my ball game!" He turns to Jack. "Hey, Dad, want to help me warm up my arm?"

Jack nods. "Sure." He kisses my forehead before following Jeff into the garage to grab their gloves and a ball.

We're home, but not for long.

20

How to Welcome Him Home

Huzzah! Your road warrior is home from his latest adventure! To make him wish he never had to leave your well-feathered nest again, here's what you should do:

First, greet him with his favorite cocktail in hand. Why give him an excuse to go out to his local bar? Learning how to mix a mean martini allows him to forget his troubles and just get happy in the comfort of his own home—and his own wife's arms.

Next, ask about his week! You'll have just as much fun listening to him regale you with his acts of derring-do in the cruel world of corporate boardrooms as he will when he hears your scintillating stories about getting the stain out of your favorite coffee table, or ignoring the plumber's ass-crack when the dishwasher went on the fritz.

And, finally, never get out of your negligee—unless it's at his personal request. Remember, your birthday suit is very,

very special to him. Look at it this way: when you're the only naked woman in the room, he only has eyes for you.

THE HEADQUARTERS OF OPERATION TEUTONIC TYRANT IS THE bonus room over the garage.

Evan doesn't mind this because it puts him in the guest room, which is next to Mary's room. He doesn't know that I've got surveillance in both, which is why my timing is always so good when their flirting inches up towards petting.

"Ah, great memories," Emma murmurs. She's being sarcastic. The last time she worked in the bonus room was when the Quorum planted a cell in Hilldale. To keep the neighbors from being suspicious of all the activity coming in and out of my home, Emma posed as my nanny. This meant a few trips to the playground with Trisha. She hated being hit on by the neighborhood DILFs.

Confirmation that Eric is back in his old stomping grounds—the French countryside—comes when one of the Quorum's Swiss bank accounts makes a deposit into a realtor's account in the little village of Vaucluse, France.

After hacking into the realtor's computer, Emma gives a long, low whistle. "Wow! About a year ago, he purchased an old Franciscan monastery that dates back to the twelve-hundreds, but it's been abandoned for at least a couple of centuries."

"Pull it up on satellite," Jack suggests.

She taps in the GPS coordinates taken from the property deed. What we see is a five-story stone monastery on a valley floor, but built into the side of a sheer cliff of the Dentelles de Montmirail Mountain Range. Old vines are entwined in its ancient columns.

"That makes sense," Dominic murmurs. "A stone fortress for a religious sect besieged by a series of unfriendly reigns would be quite naturally well reinforced against a siege by unfriendly forces."

Looking up from his computer, Arnie groans. "Folks, we've got some good news, some bad news, and some really bad news. Which one do you want first?"

Ryan throws his hands up in the air. "Start with the good, and work your way backward."

"Okay, well the good news is that when I hacked into Eileen's phone texts, I grabbed Eric's cell number, and so I was able to hack into his texts as well. The bad news is that something big is going down at his monk cave tomorrow night."

Ryan winces before asking, "And what's the really bad news?"

"It looks like it's going to be an auction of one of the implosive nuclear weapons that Eric stole from some Russian munitions arsenal. The auction is to take place three days from now."

Jack nods. "It's late evening there. Zoom in. Maybe we can get a head count of the number of goons he's got within his security detail."

Emma widens the shot on Eric's new lair and tilts the

trajectory. What once looked like ants have grown into men holding semi-automatic rifles. "At least six on the ramparts, and another six on the grounds. Interestingly enough, none on the roof."

"Its only access is a sheer cliff that rises at least eighty feet above the monastery. Eric's security team wouldn't expect entry from there," Dominic replies.

"That may work for us. Look at this." I point to a faint brown image snaking through the tree line below toward the summit of the mountain, which, unlike the other peaks, has been sheared flat by some act of nature.

Emma zooms in. "It could be some kind of trail."

"Ah! I'll wager it was the last resort for the monks, should the barbarians make it through the gates," Dominic reasons. "Can you get in closer, so that we can peruse the roof for any openings?"

Emma shifts the point-of view to the room, and zooms in even closer. As he suspects, there is a small trap door in the floor of the roof.

"Bingo," Abu exclaims.

"Emma, for the next seventy-two hours, open a screen that takes in a twenty-mile radius of the rest of the valley," I suggest.

Emma nods. "Are we looking for anything specific?"

"Limousines. They're probably bringing in the bidders."

"I'd give ten-to-one odds that a few of them were recently at the Lion's Lair summit," Abu growls.

I nod. "I'm sure Lee would appreciate that intel. With

photo surveillance, we should be able to ID some of them."

"You'll do better than that," Ryan declares. "George is waiting for your mission team on the Van Nuys tarmac. You and Jack are storming Weber's fortress. Abu and Arnie will provide backup and surveillance."

"Hey, this may be a perfect test for my surveillance mini-drones. They're the size of flies. In a place that size, we'll need eyes all over the place to find our two targets: the nuclear weapon and Eric."

Ryan nods. "Emma will feed the team TechInt from here. If Eric Webber is, in fact, holding a nuclear device, I want both him and it in custody before the auction commences."

Emma grimaces. The elevator ploy with Arnie gave her a taste of honeypot, and I guess she liked it. Hey, I can relate. But I'd certainly offer my dear friend a word of caution: *be careful what you wish for.*

"Ideally, we'll disarm it onsite. Dominic, the time you've spent on the Trident missile program's detonation boot camp is about to come in handy."

"Righto! Didn't earn that badge for nothing," Dominic quips. "I can't think of a more fitting way to put an end to Eric Weber's reign of terror."

I've yet to find out why our British colleague is just as eager as us to clap Eric in irons.

The trip will take a few hours. Plenty of time to bond.

But, first things first: Jack and I need to talk.

As the team mission leader, Jack gets dibs on the plane's bedroom suite, which means I do too. While the others—Abu, Dominic, and Arnie—settle in to watch a world soccer tournament, Jack and I flop down on our bed.

He doesn't stop me from pulling off his T-shirt in order to examine his cuts and bruises. Yes, he's on the mend, but a few of those wounds are quite deep and will take time to fully heal.

When I touch one of those, he flinches.

"I wish I had some sort of lotion, or salve, or something to help it heal…" I say, innocently enough.

Silently, he turns his head toward the wall.

Then I remember Jack and that woman on the video. "Jack, I…I love you, and I trust you. It's just that—well, the way you acted on the video with…with that woman—"

"Her name was Lola." He sounds so far away.

"Okay then, Lola. The two of you were so—so *intimate*."

He sighs as he turns to me, finally. "I killed her fiancé. She wanted to kill me for it—until she realized I had no choice in the matter. She wanted out of Paraíso as much as me. That's what brought us together. What you saw on the video—it was all for show. We knew the guards were watching us. By pretending to share our lust—not our *love* —she was able to pass me the intel I needed to break out."

He strokes my cheek. "Donna, every moment I was in captivity—my every thought, my every dream—was about you! I needed to know that you believed in your heart that I'd come home to you." He pats his chest. "I wrote you every day—in here. It was the only way I could stifle the fear that I'd never come home to you and our family. Do you know why I cut off Varick's head? Because he told me you were doing that devil Eric Weber's bidding in order to save me! That they had proof of your treason, and were going to sell it to Lee's enemies—as if you were his whore, or something." He shakes his head angrily. "I put you in that position! I let you down."

"No, Jack! You've never let me down!" I kiss his face all over. The sweet saltiness of his skin is proof that I am not dreaming now; that he truly is beside me. "Varick didn't know I'd let Ryan in on it, and therefore Lee too… that they were shadowing every assignment and flipping it to safeguard our country."

Jack shrugs. "Then I guess I was a bit hard on Lee."

"He's a big boy. He can take it." I stroke his chest gently.

"His feelings for you are much too obvious."

"Yeah, I've noticed that too. So, do what I do—*ignore them.*"

He laughs.

My God, it's been too long since I've heard that beautiful sound.

Up until a few minutes ago, I never thought I'd hear it again.

Thank you, God, for bringing him home to me.

My tears bring his laughter to a dead stop. To make things worse, I'm babbling so hard that even I can't make out what I'm saying—something to the effect of, *Please, please, never stop laughing, never stop loving me, never ever leave me again…*

He tries to shush me with whispers that tell me all I want to hear, and more: that it is our love that drives him to be the best man he can be; that he will never leave me as long as he can breathe…

To prove it, he wraps his arms tightly around me, enveloping me with warmth and desire. His heart beats so furiously in his chest that I am compelled to place my hand over it.

Jack shudders at my touch. It is a natural reaction—we both know it. But it is the wrong reaction. The last thing I want is for him to move away from me.

I want him inside of me.

When I slide his hand along my heated skin—down my side then below my abdomen—I'm acutely sensitive to the new callouses on his hands. A shiver courses over my body. I don't know if it's because I'm elated he's here touching me, or I'm terrified at what I nearly lost.

In time, his hand slips below the silky fabric of my panties to the soft mound beneath it. When his thumb and forefinger join together, their gentle nudges quicken into a single pulsating piston. I moan when his mouth finds my breast. His tongue tickles my nipple before his lips nuzzle it gently. These sensations, taken together, send all thoughts out of my brain, except for one:

We are one again.

As if reading my mind, his hands pull away, if only to suspend him over me.

When he enters me, we are eye to eye. With each thrust, his face—and mine too, I'm sure—reflect the fierce joy and sheer elation of our mutual passion.

Each groan is a testament to our timeless love.

By the time he erupts, I am already swept into a deep pool of my own emotions. I swirl through them and in them and around them until the here and now vanish into the single reality of him and me.

Finally, he collapses.

"Welcome home," I gasp.

At ten at night, we land at the Avignon-Caumont Airport, where we have a helicopter waiting for George, Dominic, Jack, and me.

Abu will be waiting for us near the monastery in an armored truck disguised as a refrigerated grocery van.

George flies toward the monastery, but on a route so circuitous that at no time can he be seen or heard by Eric's security detail as we land near the mountain's summit.

By midnight, Dominic, Jack, and I have rappelled down until we reach the monastery's roof, but stop short until we hear Arnie pronounce, "It's clear of any sensors. None on the trap door either, so go for it."

We head for the rooftop trap door that we saw on the satellite feed. It is locked from the inside. We take a crowbar to the old hinges, and in we go.

"These thick stone walls make it practically impossible for a thermal scan, but from what I'm reading, you'll find a guard on each floor's rampart, which is on the center of each hallway," Arnie informs us. "There are at least six on the ground floor, so I'd guess it's the location of their sleeping quarters. Be careful, because there may be a few wandering the halls that I can't pick up."

"Will do," Jack assures him.

With Dominic in the lead, step by step, we make our way down the stone stairwell. When we reach the fourth level, he turns a corner with me right on his heels—

Smack into Gunter.

He's got a cigarette in one hand, and a lighter in the other. Up here no one would come looking for him while he snuck off to have a smoke.

As Gunter reaches for his rifle, I hiss, "Duck," to Dominic.

The bullet from my gun pierces his forehead.

Glad I had the chance to do the honors.

Like Jack, Dominic is fluent in French. He takes Gunter's earpiece in his free ear so that he can hear any commands from the rest of the security team, and feed them back to us.

Jack motions for me to release the mini-drones from my backpack. I toss them up in the air. At first, the swarm hovers, but then it breaks off, each going in a different direction.

"Both Emma and I are on it," Arnie assures us through our earpieces. They must keep their eyes on several of the drones' monitors at once.

It takes a few minutes before Emma murmurs, "I found Eric. He's on level two, third door on the left."

"The guard's quarters are to the right, whereas the nuclear device is on the ground level, to your left. You can't miss the room, it's the only door on that level. Apparently, the floor is one large room. There are two guards stationed outside."

"Arnie, can you tell its size?"

"Almost fifty feet in depth, thirty wide."

Dominic nods. "Sounds about right."

"For transportation purposes, it is already carted on wheels," Arnie adds. "I see an elevator shaft. I guess the lucky winner can pull up to the loading dock, sort of like picking up boxed furniture from Ikea!"

"Not quite, but we get the picture," I murmur.

"On the way down, we take out the rampart guards," Jack instructs us. "Then we split up. Donna, you and Dominic will go to Level One and secure the device." He frowns. "I'll go for Eric on Level Two."

If anyone deserves the kill, it's Jack.

"Bring him back alive." Ryan's voice puts a grimace on Jack's face. "The Quorum isn't dissolved until we clean up all the loose ends. He's the only one who can help us do it."

Jack frowns, but he'll follow orders.

Or will he? With all he's been through in the past few days, I'm still trying to process the depth of his pain.

Eric may provide the key.

THE RAMPART GUARDS ARE ADMIRING THE MAGICAL CARPET of stars hovering over the French countryside when the bullets claim them. They hold cigarettes in their hands.

At least it's a quicker death than lung cancer.

When we reach Level Two, I give Jack a kiss for luck. He kisses back, and his clutch lingers. "I love you," we mouth in unison. Then we kiss again.

Dominic sighs.

He nudges me. Time to start our descent to Level One.

ONE OF THE GUARDS IN FRONT OF THE ROOM HOLDING THE nuclear device is nodding off. The other stares off into space, a scowl on his face. Is it because he's caught in a dead-end minimum wage job?

I nudge Dominic and point to Sleepy.

I get the honor of putting Grumpy out of his misery.

When the bullets hit, they slump to the floor.

The room holding the nuclear device is as large as a

ballroom. Perhaps it was the monks' mess hall, or maybe it was where they said their prayers. In any event, it is no longer a place of God. If Eric has his way, it will be the birthplace of the world's annihilation.

The device itself is encased in a glass chamber within the room.

Dominic whistles softly. "It's a W76 thermonuclear warhead."

My stomach leaps at the thought that we're standing so close to it. "How can you defuse it?"

"It works on a series of redundant locks. Unfortunately, my love, we don't have the codes. However, the MC4081-2 clocks on the device are encased in a removable foam core. I can pull it out."

"Let's go for it." I run toward the glass chamber and open the door.

Just as I go through, I hear a click. The door has shut behind me.

Oops.

I pull at the door. I guess it's the wrong thing to do because a posh British female voice proclaims, "You have thirty seconds to input the security code before succumbing to poisonous gas. Twenty-nine seconds... twenty-eight seconds...twenty-seven seconds..."

I slap the glass with an open fist. "What the hell, Dominic?"

"Ah, yes, it's a bit of a sticky wicket." He frowns. Suddenly, his eyes light up. "By Jove, I know that voice! She's one of the birds behind the counter at one of my private clubs—Raffles! Following her dream of becoming an actress, I presume—although her talents lay elsewhere, if you ask me—"

"I didn't!" I smack the wall once more.

"Twenty-two seconds…" Dominic's friend with benefits sounds practically bored. Maybe that's why he recognized her.

"Donna, hold your cell phone over the keypad," Emma suggests. "That way, I can scan it for fingerprints, and do a likely calculation from that."

I point my iPhone at the keypad.

"Sixteen seconds…fifteen seconds…fourteen seconds…thirteen seconds…"

Think happy thoughts.

I'm with Jack. We're sitting on a beautiful beach, clear blue skies overhead. He leans in. As I descend into his kiss, the waves crash over us.

"Eight seconds…seven seconds…"

Crash…

No, please no.

"Donna, try 3235552044!"

I leave the kiss for Emma's wild guess.

"You may proceed," the woman's voice purrs.

I open the door for Dominic.

He saunters to the tail end of the warhead and turns something. It allows him to loosen a bottom panel.

A moment later, he's holding a foam casing. It holds a clock.

"All's well that ends well."

The smartass.

"Donna, did you notice something familiar about the code?" Emma asks.

I think for a moment: it's my phone number.

Eric is too sick for words. I need him out of my life—*now.*

I tap Dominic on the shoulder and point up. "Get it out of here, and don't get caught, or we all fail. In the meantime, I'll find Jack."

"He'd want you to go with me—"

"Not in a million years! I've lost him once; I won't do it again." I shove him toward the hallway. "If we're not back in fifteen minutes, get George to fly you out of here with this clock."

I don't have to ask twice. He's taking the ancient stairwell two steps at a time.

Next stop: to find the bane of my existence—Eric—and my reason for living: Jack.

I'M ABOUT TO CLIMB UP TO LEVEL TWO, WHEN ARNIE mutters in my ear, "Donna, we have a situation."

"Give it to me straight."

"Jack got into Eric's private quarters, but he must have tripped an alarm of some sort because Eric has silently summoned back up. They are headed your way."

"How many?"

Four of the six on the ground level. The other two are

staying behind to watch the front entry. They've called for back-up from the rampart guards and are panicking because they're getting no answer—"

Even as he speaks, one turns the corner.

I crouch and aim—

He falls face down.

The guy behind him realizes too late that he's also in my crosshairs. Down he goes, on top of his dead colleague.

A third guy—I recognize him: it's Hugo—ducks back behind the doorway. The next thing I know, my Heckler & Koch G36C is exchanging fire with four Steyr AUG's.

"Help me out here, Arnie!" I shout over the gunfire.

"Got it, Donna! The door is almost sixteen inches of solid oak," Emma explains. "It swings shut with a pulley, which can only be opened from your side. The pulley's leverage is a net holding a boulder hanging up in the bell tower. If you can break the pulley's rope—"

"On it!" I look up. Yes, there's the rope.

I hit my attackers with enough firepower that they back off for the few seconds I need to point up at the rope.

Just as Hugo sticks out his arm to assault me with another round of bullets, the door slams shut, severing his arm from the rest of his body.

Hugo's blood-chilling scream sounds as if it's far, far away. As the arm falls to the floor, the gun is still firing. A rainbow of bullets slams the wall next to my ear.

I survived.

Has Jack?

I can't run up the stairwell fast enough.

I DON'T REALIZE UNTIL IT'S TOO LATE THAT THE STAIRWELL comes up in the center of a vast room.

Turning right, I see Jack, his gun raised in a tactical stance, darting between a row of columns in search of the man who left him for dead: Eric Weber.

Does love have its own telepathy? I've always thought so. If I'm right, it's happening now because Jack turns in my direction, his weapon drawn.

His eyes open wide in surprise at seeing me—

Then even wider in horror at…what?

Something behind me…

My head whips left to follow his stare.

Eric's arm is raised. His finger presses the trigger of his gun.

I fall face down on the floor.

The bullet whizzes over my head—

Just as another whizzes toward Eric—

Catching him in the gut. Eric gasps as he drops to the floor.

I turn to Jack.

He's fallen onto his knees. Oh my God…has he been shot?

I run to him. When I reach him, he lifts his head upward, but the look on his face is as if he's seen a ghost.

"My God, Donna—the way you fell...I thought—I thought I'd shot you!"

"What? ...No! The bullet hit Eric. At the same time, I thought his bullet hit you!"

We both turn to look for the bullet hole. Finally, we find it: embedded in one of the columns.

Jack grasps me tightly and kisses me.

"L'amour, l'amour..." Eric's voice is so faint that we barely hear it.

"Abu and Dominic rounded up what's left of Eric's goon squad and locked them in the cargo van. We've called the French Directorate of Military Intelligence and told them we have an early Bastille Day present waiting for them. They'll love the fact that some of these guys have their ISIL membership cards." Ryan informs us. "Since Eric is breathing, bring him with you to the chopper. We've got a private emergency room set up for him just south, in Marseille."

Jack takes his lips off mine, if only to say, "On it, Chief."

"You really are quite a woman." Despite having difficulty speaking, Eric is still trying to impress me. During the flight, I don't look at him, let alone speak a word to him. He ignores my silence. Instead, he rhapsodizes on and on about me, in minute detail: what he loves about my laugh, my smile, and most of all, my extermination process.

Truly, one sick bastard!

I thought that even before he starts describing the way I sleep: my sighs, my moans, my twists and my turns... how I prefer the fetal position.

How I sleep in the nude.

When his rant moves on to the curvature of my silhouette, Jack pulls out his gun and holds it to Eric's temple. "I'm in the mood for Russian Roulette. Although, I have to warn you, I always play with a full deck, and I always pack an extra mag."

Eric shuts up.

I take it as proof that he doesn't really want to die.

Good. Maybe he'll cooperate with the CIA.

Not that it will buy him his freedom.

Nothing will, as long as Jack and I are alive.

When we land, his stretcher is wheeled into the elevator taking him to the private apartment that is an Acme safe house. As promised, Acme's Parisian on-call doctor is already there, and prepped for the surgery that will remove the bullet from his spleen.

Because it hit a non-vital organ, he'll live. Whether he'll spill his guts is another question altogether.

Extraordinary rendition should loosen his tongue for a whole different reason.

"I CAN TAKE IT FROM HERE." RYAN'S DECLARATION ON THE tarmac at the Marseille airport is the second surprise we get when we arrive.

The first is that he's there at all.

Jack and I look at each other. I shrug. "Okay, sure. Should we catch a ride home with you on Air George?" That's our subtle way of asking if we're supposed to fly home via commercial jet.

Ryan grins broadly. "What's you're rush? Aunt Phyllis is holding down the fort, right? Since you're already here, why not take in the sights of the French Riviera? Consider it a somewhat belated and well deserved honeymoon." He grins. "In fact, bill it to me. I'll write it off as a bonus."

Jack and I look at each other and then back to Ryan. My eyes open wide. "Really, Ryan? That would be…wonderful!"

My fantasy of Jack and I making love on some exotic beach is finally about to come true.

So is my dream that our lives will finally be without the Quorum.

We are walking out the door when Ryan's phone buzzes. It's Abu. From the look on Ryan's face, something serious is going down.

I'm almost afraid to ask, but I have to: "What's wrong?"

He waves me off. "I'll be right there," he says into his phone. Turning to us, he replies, "Eric just went into shock. But before he did, he said something strange about Babette and…Carl."

Carl?

Do I really want to hear this?

Jack grabs my hand and drags me toward the door. "You can tell us all about it when we get back, in say, two or three weeks."

He really is the man of my dreams.

I love being Mrs. Jack Craig.

—THE END—

Next Up: Excerpt

THE HOUSEWIFE ASSASSIN'S GHOST PROTOCOL (BOOK 13)

Nobody wants to drop dead.

And yet, for some odd reason, the rest of us are all the more upset when someone young and gorgeous is "taken before her time."

"Why her?" we lament. "She had her whole life ahead of her!"

True that...

Guess not.

On the upside, she also avoided wrinkling and withering into a little old lady—not to mention having her spouse leave her for some young chippy.

She will not feel dismayed on birthdays by those who patronizingly proclaim, brightly if not sincerely, "You don't look a day over (fill in the blank) ha, ha! Everyone, let's give her a big hand..."

I purposely mix metaphors when I say "age before swine."

Should you have the choice to either flame out as a bright young thing, or age honestly and gracelessly, do yourself a favor: choose the latter.

Truth is, the longer they know you, the harder it is to forget you—and that's your true endgame, isn't it?

Dying young is SO overrated.

"Quit gawking." I don't have to move my sunglasses, let alone open my eyes, to chastise my husband, Jack.

"Why would you even assume I'm staring?" Hearing his deep chuckle, I suppress a grin. His question serves as a challenge.

Game on.

"We're on a beach in Biarritz," I remind him. "Of course you're staring at *someone*. Someone who is more than likely topless." With my eyes still closed, I point toward our left. "*C'est-là.*"

Jack shifts in his lounge chair so that he can lift the brim of my hat in order to stare down at me. "How the hell did you know?"

Before opening my eyes, I sigh, then remove my sunglasses and look left.

As I suspected, three comely *filles*, perhaps nineteen or twenty years old, lay on beach blankets a few yards away. One is on her back. Her naked breasts are already reddened by the glaring sun. Another is on her side. The plum of her comely backside, topped with a tramp stamp of entwined hearts and split by a thong, is pointed in our direction.

The third girl, a waifish gamine with white blond hair and a deep tan, is raised in a cobra pose on her beach blanket. Her naked breasts, now gravitationally erect, resemble over-inflated zeppelins flying in tandem.

Even our nineteen year-old cabana boy, Jean-Pierre, pauses the vigorous shaking of our mid-day martini in order to hear my answer.

In all honesty, I had a fifty-fifty chance that Jack was looking left as opposed to right. Luck of the draw. Not that I'll willingly admit it. "Simple deduction. You've been too quiet for much too long. At the same time you haven't turned a page in your book."

"It's *Moby Dick*. It takes at least an hour to fathom each damn paragraph."

"Liar. You were reading—and I use that term lightly—the latest swimsuit edition of *Sports Illustrated*." I glance in the direction of Jean-Pierre. "Admit I'm right, or else I'll ask our manservant to give me another massage."

"Busted," Jack's reluctant apology comes with a sly grin. "Sorry. Poor choice of words."

"I'll write it off to topless-of-mind awareness." I lower my shades so that he can see my wink.

"You know, you could cut me some slack." He too nods toward Jean-Pierre.

I don't mind that Jack thinks the kid has a crush on

me. But I know it's because I'm a good tipper, so I shrug. "Done. I do concede, however, that prime beefcake trumps three cream puffs any day."

Up until now, Jean-Pierre has been ignoring the girls. French society's blasé attitude toward nudity has made him immune to their all too obvious attributes. But now that he's taken a better look at them, his face turns bright red—to my relief, not because I've embarrassed him. "*Merde*! The one at the far end—she is Nicolette Beauchamp!"

"Who?" I ask.

"I am sorry." He shakes off his anger. "She is…an old friend of mine."

As red as his face just turned, I'm sure she is more than that to him still.

He answers my questioning eyes with a shrug. "A long time ago. We were merely *enfants*. In the meantime we've grown up, and apart." He shifts his gaze in her direction. His longing is all too obvious. "Her mother is Martine, a chambermaid here at the hotel. Should she see Nicolette sunbathing *sans un maillot de bain*, she will be—how do you say…livid? Our hotelier looks down his nose on any impertinence from the staff or their families. The guests…" He bites his lips. "Well, one may get the wrong idea, *n'est-ce pas*?"

I nod. "To put it mildly. I know I'd feel the same way if it were my daughter."

Jack picks up a pair of binoculars. "Looks like we have company."

He's right. Just beyond Nicolette yet another super-yacht is jockeying for position amongst the many that dot the calm turquoise waters just a few hundred feet from these golden shores. At four hundred or more feet in length and six bridges high, the ship could be mistaken for a small aircraft carrier, easily dwarfing the other behemoths around it. The bow of the lower bridge has been hollowed out, exposing a swimming pool surrounded by chaises and an outdoor bar.

Scrolled on the stern is its name—*Divide and Conquer*—and its homeport: Antibes.

Jean-Pierre frowns. I can barely make out what he mutters under his breath. However, the phrases *"brûle en l'enfer,"* *"fils de pute,"* and that classic standby, *"merde,"* are all recognizable.

I feel my brow arching. "I take it you know the yacht's owner."

"Oui, Madame. He is a very wealthy Saudi Arabian.'" His sneer comes with an eye roll. "He built that monstrosity over there." He points to a mansion on a cliff over a strip of beach on the right of us.

I shake my head in awe. "Interesting. And I thought that was just another hotel!" An honest mistake, considering that it is larger than any other structure flanking the beach.

"If only, Madame. The citizenry of our little town is... how do you say in English...'up in arms' because he has requisitioned the beach in front of it for his private use.

He has an entourage of over a thousand friends and family."

"It looks as if his security detail is a third of it." Jack gazes at the empty wedge of beach sprawled under the rocky shoreline. A battalion of guards are lined up, perpendicular to the shoreline. If anyone attempts to go around them, they are shooed away with batons.

One of the girls—Thong—has also noticed the yacht. She nudges Nipples, who then sits up straight.

The tweet of a cell phone sends Nicolette rolling onto her back. She reaches for her beach bag and reads her text, then raises her sunglasses above her eyes in order to scrutinize the yacht's crew as they ready the onboard helicopter for their boss, a broad-shouldered man in a suit. The whirlwind caused by the helicopter's rotating rudders cause his keffiyeh to flap around his shoulders, but it doesn't deter him from texting on his cell phone.

Nicolette and he seem to tap off simultaneously. The reason for this becomes obvious when she waves at the copter as it hovers over her—and us—before alighting on the concrete deck adjacent to the cordoned-off sand.

She doesn't rise to greet him. Instead, she waits for one of his cronies to fetch her and her friends. Before sashaying off, she tosses on a tight T-shirt. Then she turns and smiles at Jean-Pierre.

He drops his head in defeat.

Nipples follows her. Thong, however, hesitates. She glances over at Jean-Pierre and blushes. Noting his scowl, she still blows him a kiss.

"She's quite beautiful," I point out.

"Gigi Marchand likes to pretend that she is in love with me," Jean-Pierre mutters. "Nicolette and the other girl—Suzette Caron—encourage it."

"And you don't want to play along?" Jack counters.

A ghost of a smile alights on Jean-Pierre's lips. Still, he shakes his head. "We all have our fantasies, eh?" His eyes are drawn to Nicolette and her lover.

So are everyone else's on the beach, for good reason. Their embrace is so erotic that heads of passersby seem to pivot a full three hundred and sixty degrees.

The man finally lets her go in order to lead her and her friends toward the helicopter.

"They aren't going into the grand villa?" I murmur to Jean-Pierre.

Jean-Pierre shakes his head adamantly. "He would not want his mistress to run into his wife. The yacht is his domain solely. "

"What did you say his name was?" Jack asks.

Jean-Pierre mutters, "al-Sadah."

Jack turns toward me. His stare mirrors mine. Salem Rahmin al-Sadah was a recent titular head of the Quorum, a terrorist funding organization.

He is also recently dead—thanks to *moi*.

Trust me, I had good cause to take him out. He'd plotted to infiltrate an anti-terrorism summit hosted by the president of the United States, Lee Chiffray, in order to murder those in his region who seek peace.

He also tried to rape me on the eve of my wedding. I'd say I owed him a very long good-bye.

Salem could not have survived it. I know, because I watched him die.

Jack lays his hand on my arm. "Probably a brother, or a cousin. Remember, it's a big family."

I shiver, not because of any chill—after all, the sun shines overhead—but because it felt as if someone walked across my grave.

Or crawled out of one.

Just then, the helicopter takes off. It swoops low over us before arcing back over the water toward the yacht.

In its wake, my sunhat flies off, skipping over the sand before landing in the tide.

It floats downstream, toward al-Sadah's palace.

"Oh, hell," I mutter. "It was my favorite. Now it's ruined."

Jack laughs as he takes me by my wrists in order to lift me off my chaise. "Don't worry. I'll buy you a new one— but not now. It's siesta time."

This is code for our afternoon delight. It is part of a daily ritual.

Our hotel was once a private villa. Its greatest feature is that it is small in comparison to the others along the beach, and that it has a handful of private cabanas stag- gered along the beach.

Ours juts out over the ocean. During high tide, when the waves slap against the pylons beneath our room, we feel as if we're floating out on the sea.

A large round bed is centered in the room, which is glassed in on three sides. Two face either end of the beach, while the third affords us a straight-on ocean view.

Wall-to-ceiling drapes give us complete privacy from the beach sides, if that is what we desire. We've yet to open them. Needless to say, we've been sleeping like newborns, partying like co-eds during Spring Break, and making love like the newlyweds we are.

So then, why do I feel as if our honeymoon is over?

"You're not here with me," Jack murmurs, despite the fact that I am nestled, naked, in the crook of his arm.

As usual, his intuition is spot on. My mind is a million miles away—in this case, the Beverly Wilshire on the day of my rendezvous with Salem Rahmin al-Sadah. My game plan was to retrieve intel secreted in his ring bearing the crest of the Quorum. His was to dominate me into sexual submission.

I got the ring. He got a bullet to the heart.

Now, I wonder: did Salem survive my kill shot? And, if so, how?

Under normal circumstances, post-coitus isn't the best time for post-op analysis. Still, Jack asked, so in for a dime, in for a dollar. "Hearing the name al-Sadah spooked me, I guess." I lift my head so that I can gauge his reaction to what I say next. "Jack, don't you find it strange that

Salem's death was never made public? Why have we never heard a word about it?"

"Acme cleaned up behind us." Hearing the wariness in my tone, he adds, "Would it make you feel better if I called Ryan to confirm?"

"No, no—don't! I mean…well, we've been gone almost two weeks now, and we've held to our vow to stay away from work and home." By the time I've flipped over onto his chest, I've got a smile on my face. "I guess I'm a little bored…not to mention homesick."

Hearing this, his left brow almost hits the ceiling. "Oh, really? Despite having all of Hilldale on twenty-four hour surveillance?"

Okay, he's right. As far as my three children are concerned, I've not exactly gone dark. I'm monitoring Mary, Jeff, and Trisha's comings and goings, as well as those of our legal ward, Evan Martin.

"A parent can never be too diligent." Even to my own ears, my retort sounds a bit defensive. To make my point, I add, "Have you forgotten they're with Aunt Phyllis? It's akin to leaving the craziest inmate in charge of the asylum!"

Jack shrugs. "Granted, she's been lax about the amount of TV they watch, and the number of video games they're allowed to play—"

"To say nothing about late bedtimes and the number of sleepovers she's allowed," I remind him. "Our home is now Hilldale's teen party central! And let's face it: she turns a blind eye to the obvious attraction between Mary and Evan. Since we've been gone, their flirting has become a full-court press."

"Donna, doll, you're jumping to all kinds of unfounded conclusions—"

"Unfounded?" It's my turn to hike a brow. "They've been sneaking off to the playhouse in the back. It's the only place on the property that doesn't have a webcam." Suddenly, I sit straight up in bed. "Oh, my God! There's a bed in there! Granted, it's only a twin—"

He pulls me back down into his arms. Gently, he puts a finger against my lips. "It's only natural that they feel empathy toward each other. They've both suffered public humiliations: parents who committed heinous crimes, as well as the personal tragedies of a parent's death. In Evan's case, both his father and mother. How many kids their age can say that?"

I flinch, knowing that my mother's fight with terminal breast cancer still haunts me. I was only eleven when she died.

Noting my reaction, Jack traces the curve of my face with his index finger. He has always been tender with me after lovemaking. But since his escape from Mexico, sadness deepens his already dark green eyes.

I concede with a nod. "You're right. I'm overreacting. I guess I'm antsy because I'm not use to just being...well, *happy*." I sigh. "I'm always waiting for the other shoe to drop."

Jack's kidnapping, on the night of our nuptials, almost killed us, and I mean that quite literally. While his sadistic captor pitted him in a series of death matches against other prisoners, I was at the beck and call of another of the Quorum's notorious leaders, Eric Weber.

Eric promised to release Jack if I followed through on a series of tasks that, when completed, would have marked me as a domestic terrorist. I did the tasks, but I had help. My team at Acme Industries shadowed my every move so that any intel I passed was black propaganda, and the kidnapping of an aeronautic scientist working on a top secret government project was extracted into WITSEC—the US Marshall's Witness Security Program.

Granted, there was one screw-up: my final mission was to exterminate my boss, Ryan Clancy.

Eric's directive was delivered at a time when I was naked, both in the Biblical sense and in the vernacular of our business—that is to say, I had no backup, and therefore no way to warn Ryan that I'd be gunning for him.

To save Jack, the hit had to take place.

So, yeah, I killed my boss and mentor.

As it turns out, Acme had my room bugged. Without my knowledge, Ryan's death was faked. I would say "all's well that ends well" except for the fact that despite jumping through all those hoops, I still almost lost Jack, both physically and emotionally.

Never again.

"I'll be damned if I'm going to spend the rest of our honeymoon reliving the worst day of our lives." If Jack's vow echoes my very thoughts, his actions speak louder than words. He kisses me: first, fiercely; but soon his actions become a drawn out achingly gentle game of touch and feel.

He's in it to win it.

He gains big points as his lips slide down my neck and between my breasts. There, he pauses for a moment. His eyes shifting to my right breast, then to the left, like a kid who has landed on a Candy Land game board and doesn't know which way to turn.

The left proves the luckier of the two.

His mouth seems to swallow it whole. Instinctively, I brace for the tingle due to come from the feel of his tongue on my nipple. Soon, I'm moaning from the pleasure of his touch. But in no time he has circled back down into the valley of my bosom and over to my right breast, licking my nipple until it too goes taut.

His lips meander. The stubble on his cheek tickles the slight swell of my belly. He takes my frenzied groan as the signal to quit teasing me.

He's right. It's time for the main event.

As Jack enters me, his body, cantilevered by his thick muscled arms, hovers over mine.

His eyes open wide in rapturous adoration. The late afternoon sun's rays, streaming through the undulating curtains, fan out behind his head, crowning him with a halo.

Am I imagining it? No. He is my protector.

The one true love of my life.

My angel.

His thrusts, steady and deep, fill my heart with joy. As

Jack's ecstasy swells within me, all thoughts scatter from my mind, like crispy leaves whipped out of reach by a brisk autumn gale.

Finally, spent, he shudders as he collapses onto me.

We lay there for some time, chest to breast. His heart pulsates in tandem with mine.

As it should be.

Always.

If only.

A scream wakes us from our post-coital slumber.

The wailing doesn't stop, but only gets louder, more agitated. A moment later, voices are raised in raucous accusations.

The chorus of shouts also gets louder as time goes by.

Jack groans. Still, he unfurls his arms and legs from me in order to ease himself from our bed. His small nod to modesty is to open the curtain only partially, in order to view the ruckus.

It is evening. Right now the only light is coming off the super yachts. The glow, mirrored in still waters, casts long shadows on the man who still thrills me. It darkens his soulful eyes, heightens his cheekbones, and etches the sinews of his muscular physique. If his curls were alabaster instead of naturally dark brown, I'd swear he was a sculpture by Michelangelo.

My newly piqued lust quickly dissipates under the

singsong blare of police sirens. I leap out of bed, too, scooping up a fallen robe and wrapping it around me before joining Jack at the window.

From what I can tell, a crowd has gathered on the beach a mere hundred yards from our terrace. Police officers seem to have taken control, shooing away the gawkers.

"A drowning?" I wonder out loud.

I've barely had time to take note of the action when we hear a rap on our door. I tie my robe tight around my middle while Jack slips into loose sweat pants and a T-shirt. When I see he's fully clothed, I open the door.

Two policemen face us. Jean-Pierre stands between them. He is wet and smeared with sand. Tears and fear brighten his red-rimmed eyes.

What the hell is going on?

"*Oui, les agents*?" Jack's nonchalance doesn't betray his own shock and awe.

As he asks, the nose of the older and bulkier of the two officers twitches. Perhaps he has noted our post-coital musk. "*Pardonnez-nous,* Monsieur and Madame Craig. May we have a moment of your time?" Switching to English is a courtesy proffered by most public servants along the French coastline, which is heavily trafficked by British and American tourists.

"But of course." Having lived in this country for many years, Jack's French is excellent, but for my benefit, he responds likewise. He leans forward in order to read the officer's nametag. Noting it, he nods. "How may we help you, Captain Duclos?"

The younger officer hides his smirk in a cough. Perhaps it has something to do with Jack's generous promotion for his partner, a mere beat cop.

"Jean-Pierre Gambon claims he has spent the last few hours here, with you. Can you confirm this?" Duclos's way to silence Jean-Pierre before he says anything is to clamp his hand so hard on our cabana boy's shoulder that he winces.

Jack looks to me, then to Jean-Pierre.

Jean-Pierre's eyes say it all: *Help me.*

Before Jack opens his mouth, I purr, "He gives wonderful massages, Captain. You should try one some time."

Duclos's response to my suggestion is a wary glare. "This is not a joking matter, Madame. Jean-Pierre was found on the beach, clinging to the body of a dead woman: Nicolette Beauchamp."

Jack's smile fades. "But—if she has drowned, why detain Jean-Pierre?"

Duclos shakes his head. "Drowned? *Non.* She was strangled. The coroner will soon determine the time of death." Duclos turns to me. "I ask you again, Madame: when exactly did you receive your massage?"

Jean-Pierre's mouth gapes open, but nothing comes out. His eyes implore me to save him.

To believe him.

For some reason, I do. When Jean-Pierre looked at Nicolette, his eyes were filled with adoration. With love.

And, sadly, regret.

He has so much more to regret now.

"Jack's massage was first. It ran over an hour, didn't it, Jack?" I turn innocently to my husband.

His eyebrow arches. Still, he nods his head. "Yours was immediately afterward. And about the same amount of time." His tone leaves no room for doubt.

The younger officer takes a pad from his pocket and scribbles this down.

Duclos scowls. "Again, Monsieur, what time were these massages?"

"Well…" Jack looks skyward, as if searching his memory. "Jean-Pierre left only, say, a half hour before the sirens began."

"And only because I asked him to walk out onto the beach. I'd misplaced my sun hat. It's black, with a white band around the rim," I add. I tilt my head in Jean-Pierre's direction. "By the way, did you find it?"

Slowly, Jean-Pierre shakes his head. Still stunned, he says nothing.

Inspector Duclos is no idiot. He realizes his number one suspect has not just one alibi, but two. His grip loosens on Jean-Pierre. With a tip to the brim of his hat, he growls, "Good night, Madame and Monsieur."

"Wait! Officer, aren't you going to ask us what we might know about Nicolette's whereabouts?"

This stops Duclos in his tracks. "*Oui*, Madame. And what may that be?"

"Late this afternoon, the young lady was sunbathing beside us, along with two of her friends. When a humongous yacht dropped anchor, they ran over to the owner's helicopter and flew back to it with him—what is his name again? You know, the Middle-Eastern gentleman that owns the big pink monstrosity on the hill?"

The color drains from Duclos's face. "Salem al-Sadah?"

So, it is Salem after all.

But how could that be?

"Yes, that's the man," I assure him. "She welcomed him on the beach. Everyone around saw it. In fact, she was talking to him on his phone as his helicopter landed beside us. I remember this because I lost my hat because of it."

"I'm sure what my wife said can be verified by Mademoiselle Beauchamp's cell phone records," Jack adds. "Since Mr. al-Sadah may have been the last person to see her alive, why don't you start your investigation there?"

Duclos's lips pucker at this new information, and no wonder. If what Jean-Pierre said earlier—that the local police are paid to look the other way at al-Sadah's indiscretions—I assume he's not too eager to poke at that bear.

Well, too bad. It beats blaming an innocent man.

Finally, Duclos shrugs. "The gentleman is having a private party on his yacht, as we speak. A masked ball!

But of course tomorrow morning we will inquire as to any such rendezvous."

"Mr. al-Sadah does not like to be bothered before noon," Duclos's partner reminds him. "In fact, the captain mentioned that the *Divide and Conquer* leaves port early in the morning."

His honesty earns him a scowl from Duclos.

"Seriously, you're just going to let him float away?" I taunt him. "You have a dead woman on your hands—for that matter, maybe more than one. Nicolette's friends accompanied her and al-Sadah. Have you questioned them? What will you do if two more bodies end up on the beach?"

"If you're implying that Mr. al-Sadah had anything to do with this tragedy, I assure you, Madame, nothing could be further from the truth."

Jack steps so close to Duclos that they are face to face. "You don't know if you don't ask."

Shame rises in a red blush on Duclos's face. Still, he says nothing.

"If you'll excuse us, now, it's the cocktail hour." Jack nods toward the suite's fully stocked bar. He takes out a twenty-euro note and sticks it in top left pocket of Duclos's jacket. "Thanks for returning our cabana boy. If we can think of anything else you may want to ignore, we'll be sure to give you a call."

I link one arm into Jean-Pierre's in order to draw him inside the room. The other arm firmly closes the door behind us.

"They thought I killed Nicolette. Don't they realize…" Jean-Pierre stares at the door as if he expects the long arm of the law to punch its way back in and pull him out.

"That you love her? A crime of passion always provides a possible suspect, Jean-Pierre. But you didn't kill her." Jack's tone insists that Jean-Pierre confirm this.

"*Mais non*, Monsieur! You must believe me!"

I pat his arm. "We do, Jean-Pierre. And since we are now your official alibi, you must tell us the truth about your whereabouts since we left you this afternoon, up until you were found with Nicolette on the beach."

He thinks for a moment. "The concierge told me there had been a request I retrieve the suitcase for another guest from his room and take it to the luggage room. The man was checking out soon. When I took the bag from him, I mentioned I was also the hotel's masseur. He asked that I accommodate him after dropping off the bag. Of course, I did."

"Then this guest could contradict us as to your whereabouts," I point out.

"No! He has…what I mean to say is…" He runs his fingers through his thick curly blond hair. "He will be… discreet. He has too much to lose."

"I see."

Jean-Pierre shakes his head. "It is not what you think at all! You see, he too does not want others to know he is here. He is spying on his wife, who is here with her lover." He shrugs. "Then again, he was here with his lover."

"How very French," I murmur.

"Not at all," Jean-Pierre replies. "From his accent, he could be Austrian."

The joke is on me, I guess. "What is the man's name?"

"Smith. John Smith."

"An old Austrian moniker if I ever heard one." Jack shakes his head. "How did you end up on the beach beside the body?"

"After Monsieur Smith's massage, his lover requested one as well. In the meantime, he went for a walk on the beach. When he returned he realized he'd taken off his sunglasses while watching the sunset. Because they were running late to catch their flight, he asked me to retrieve them. I found them a few meters from where Nicolette lay." He takes the glasses out of his pocket and holds them up. "I would have mentioned them to the police, but while I was being questioned, I noticed their limousine drive off." He hesitates then adds, "It was an imposition to use your names, but I had no choice! You can see this, *oui*?"

"*Oui*," I mutter. "How convenient that his glasses were practically in the exact spot as Nicolette's body."

Jean-Pierre's eyes open wide. "Do you believe he had anything to do with her death?"

"It is an obvious coincidence," Jack concedes. "Tell us, Jean-Pierre: what did Monsieur Smith look like?"

Jean-Pierre thinks a moment. "He is a short man, and almost bald. His manner is a bit nervous. Surprisingly, despite the temperature, he chose to wear a wool suit. He also wears glasses—the ones that are circular in shape and tortoise shell in style."

At that moment, there is a knock on the door.

I open it. A bellhop hands me a suitcase. *"Pour Monsieur Craig. Compliments d'un vieil ami."*

"This was sent from an old friend?" I turn to Jack. "But no one knows we're here. Were you expecting anything?"

He shakes his head.

The bellhop shrugs and walks away, leaving me holding the bag.

And it's ticking.

What the…

Jack hears it too. He grabs it out of my hand and runs toward the door leading out onto the terrace.

Shocked, I watch as he slings the case with all his might toward the sea.

It drops into the water—

Just in the nick of time. Still, the explosion deafens us.

A tidal wave hits us. Jean-Pierre and I are thrown backward, like rag dolls.

My head slams into the wall. Before I pass out, the last thing I remember is Jack flying through the air toward me.

My angel.

Other Books by Josie Brown

The True Hollywood Lies Series

Hollywood Hunk

Hollywood Whore

The Totlandia Series

The Onesies - Book 1 (Fall)

The Onesies - Book 2 (Winter)

The Onesies - Book 3 (Spring)

The Onesies - Book 4 (Summer)

The Twosies - Book 5 (Fall)

The Twosies – Book 6 (Winter)

The Twosies - Book 7 (Spring)

The Twosies - Book 8 (Summer)

More Josie Brown Novels

The Candidate

Secret Lives of Husbands and Wives

The Baby Planner

How to Reach Josie

To write Josie, go to:
mailfromjosie@gmail.com

To find out more about Josie, or to get on her eLetter list
for book launch announcements, go to her website:
www.JosieBrown.com

You can also find her at:

www.AuthorProvocateur.com

twitter.com / JosieBrownCA

facebook.com / josiebrownauthor

pinterest.com / josiebrownca

instagram.com / josiebrownnovels